a *Songbird* novel

rough water

MELISSA PEARL

ISBN: 1533316287
ISBN-13: 978-1533316288

<u>NOTE</u>

For the last six Songbird Novels, I have placed the playlist here, but one reader suggested to me that I should put it in the back, as the song list can give too much away. So that's what I've done. If you'd like to see it first, you are welcome to follow flick to the end of the book to check it out.

For Jason Mraz

Your songs and voice touch my heart. Thank you for inspiring me with your beautiful, creative, intelligent music. You'll forever be one of my favorite artists.

ONE

SARAH

"I now pronounce you husband and wife." The minister smiled between us then winked at Justin. "You may kiss your bride."

Bubbles made up of giggles and fairy dust rose and popped inside me. I was positive I'd never been so happy in my entire life. Justin smiled down at me, his gentle eyes bathing me in his warmth and devotion. He was the best man I'd ever met. Yes, even better than my dad. From that first night we met and stayed up talking until four in the morning, I knew I'd love him for the rest of my life. Dating him was easy. Being with him was natural.

So far, there'd been nothing hard or complicated about our relationship.

I could say with certainty that nothing would ever break us. Our marriage was going to be perfect.

Justin's arm slipped around my waist, and he pulled me toward him. Gliding my fingers around his neck, I relished the touch of his hand on my cheek. His thumb rested on my jawline as he tipped my head back and met my lips.

People started clapping as soon as our mouths touched, but it was white noise—a distant sound that couldn't breach our moment.

Justin skimmed his nose against mine before pulling back. His eyes glistened as he mouthed the words, "I love you."

I smiled so wide my face hurt then turned to the guests and shouted, "I'm Mrs. Doyle!"

Raucous laughter was followed by a loud cheer while Justin blushed and wrapped his arm around my waist.

People called me Sparkles—it was a nickname my dad gave me because whenever I smiled, my eyes seemed to glitter like the stars. I'm pretty sure my eyes were acting like supernovas that day.

"Angel" by Casting Crowns started playing through the sound system. I grinned at Justin then followed my best friend, Jane, and Justin's brother, Blake, behind the altar so we could sign our marriage certificate.

The wedding was taking place in my family church. It was a massive building with huge glass windows that let in copious amounts of light. The modern decor was all straight lines and clean edges. Not my first choice, but my parents really wanted me to get married there, and I was too excited to be wedding the man of my dreams to put up any kind of fight.

"Selfie," Justin whispered, gently nudging my arm and lifting the phone above us. I did a cheesy grin while people in the congregation tittered at our antics. Justin took two pictures then slid the phone back into his pocket.

Still grinning, I rested my head on his shoulder while Jane signed her name on the documents. It would take a lot to extinguish my smile. I was pretty sure I'd be living with a permanent grin from this day forward. My cheeks were hurting, but I didn't care.

"This is the best day ever," I murmured to my husband. Eeekkk! My husband!

He kissed my hair and squeezed my hand. We watched Blake shift around Jane and lean over the white table to sign the documents. The emerald engagement ring on Jane's finger glittered under the lights. She and Blake were actually engaged before us, but Justin's big brother insisted we marry first. It was the sweetest gesture. The couple told us we could have the first wedding, under the condition that at the end of our two-week honeymoon, we met them in England to attend their summer ceremony. It was an easy sell.

Blake scribbled his name then winked at me, flashing me one of his brilliant smiles. I'd grown up with three older sisters. They all had partners now, but none of them felt like brothers...not the way Blake did.

The four of us were a little family unit. Until a week ago, we'd all been living in the same house, ten minutes from the Stanford University campus. College brought us together, and nothing could break that bond. It wouldn't surprise me if Jane and Blake ended up moving from Palo Alto to LA. We could find houses on the same street. Better yet, we could start having babies around the same time and grow our family even bigger.

*****

I brushed my hands down my cream and gold dress then swiveled to check out the back in the mirror. Man, I loved this wedding dress. It was the first one I'd ever made. I designed it for my final college assignment, knowing I'd be wearing it soon after graduation.

I received the highest mark I ever had, and the dress scored me an interview at Echelon Fashion. I started a week after my honeymoon. Talk about things falling into place. Mom and Dad were letting Justin and me live in one of their houses for minimal rent. It was in the Pacific Palisades, which we'd never be able to afford normally. I'd scored the dream job at a company I'd been admiring for years, and I'd just married the perfect man. Life was good!

"You nearly ready?" Jane popped her head into

the hotel bathroom. "I think they're about to start the first dance."

"Okay." I grinned, the bubbles inside me still going crazy. I was a champagne bottle, overflowing with excitement…a giddy girl who couldn't wipe the smile off her face. My cheeks were going to be so sore the next day, but it didn't matter. I was Mrs. Doyle. Nothing else mattered but that.

I ran my finger under my lips and brushed my cheeks before gently repositioning the sparkly headband I'd made to go with the dress.

"You look gorgeous. Come on."

I took Jane's outstretched hand, and we bustled to the ballroom. Her long dress swished across the carpet, and I checked the back to make sure it was still sitting straight. I'd made all the bridesmaids' dresses as well. It had been a labor of love…passion. Designing and creating clothes had been my greatest joy for as long as I could remember. Wedding outfits were my favorite.

I let go of Jane's hand and straightened one of the crisscross straps across her shoulders. That was better.

She spun with a knowing grin. "Would you stop fussing. The dresses are perfect. This night is perfect. Everything you did has made it spectacular." Holding my shoulders, she bent down and gave me a loving kiss on the cheek. "You were born to create magic like this, and I can't wait to see you do it all over again in a couple of weeks."

It was her turn to be giddy. Her pale cheeks

flushed pink as her green eyes shone.

I held her elbows and jumped up on my tiptoes. "July is like the best month ever!"

"Totally!" She dipped her knees then wrapped me in a hug.

"Love you, Janey."

"Love you too, Sparks."

"All right, all right, that's enough with the hugging. You're gonna make each other cry and then makeup will run. It won't be pretty." Blake sauntered up behind his fiancée.

I pulled away from her and giggled, dabbing beneath my eyes to make sure I still looked presentable. Blake ran his hand lightly up Jane's long neck, gazing down at her with unchecked affection. I knew that look. Justin gave it to me every day.

"Justin's going nuts waiting for you to get back." Blake pointed at the double doors behind us.

"How can you tell?" I grinned.

"His eyebrow's twitching."

I tipped my head back with a laugh. Justin was an expert at keeping the big feels on the down-low. He let me and Blake in, but when it came to the rest of the world, his guard was secure and his emotions in check. I'd never seen him lose his temper or raise his voice...or even cry. The only thing to give away his stress was his stutter that tended to appear whenever he got really nervous...or tired.

Thankfully, he'd breezed through his wedding day so far. A couple of little trip-ups during his wedding speech, but as soon as he turned to face me, it disappeared.

I loved that I could bring out the calm in him.

Slipping past my best friends, I headed back into the ballroom, swishing around tables and stopping to say hello to various guests.

"Your dress is divine."

"You look stunning."

"Such a talented girl."

"I'm so happy for you, dear."

I thanked each person as I worked my way through the room, my eyes seeking Justin the whole time. He was at the head table, chatting with my sister, Maria. He kept glancing over his shoulder, no doubt looking for me. I shuffled to the left, so I'd be in his line of sight next time he looked across.

"There's my girl." Dad's deep voice caught my attention.

"Hey, Daddy." I rose to my tiptoes and gave him a kiss.

He smiled down at me. His ever-present pride was touched with a sad nostalgia.

"Daddy," I chided. "You promised."

"I know." He sniffed. "I just can't believe my baby's gotten herself hitched."

"To a wonderful man." I rested my hand on his broad chest. It looked so tiny sitting against the white square in his breast pocket.

I had always been Daddy's precious baby girl, the youngest in the pack, and he never wanted me to leave the nest. He was a powerful man who ran his own record company. He was used to getting what he wanted. Letting me go had never been on his radar, and he'd struggled to do it.

However, in the last few months, he'd stepped up and really shown himself to be the father I adored. He'd offered Justin a position at Torrence Records working in the law department. Justin would study for his law degree part time while gaining experience working for my father. They'd also offered us the house in Pacific Palisades. It was a huge sign of respect, and Justin had said yes without hesitation.

Things had fallen into place perfectly.

Justin's eyes locked onto me. I could feel his gaze and turned to smile at him. His eyes skittered over my dad before coming back to me.

"I'm going to go have my first dance now," I murmured.

"Okay, Sparkles. But I get the next one."

"I'll be looking for ya." I winked.

He chuckled then looked over the tables and raised his hand at the MC. The mic came on and a smooth voice wafted over the crowd. "Okay, folks, it's time for the first dance. I believe Justin has hand-picked this song for his lady love."

I stopped on the edge of the dance floor, anticipation firing through me as Justin's shoes echoed on the shiny wood. Taking my hand, he raised it to his lips as "She's Got A Way" by Billy Joel filtered into the room.

Aw, of course he did.

Justin was a man of few words, but he always

found the best songs to tell me what his heart was really saying.

My giggle was soft and breathy as he gently tugged me onto the floor. He lifted his arm, and I spun beneath it. My dress floated out like a Cinderella ball gown before he pulled me back against him. His solid chest pressed against mine as his arms wrapped around my waist, holding me safe and secure. I gazed into his eyes. The bubbles inside were overflowing. My eyes glistened as I swayed against him and listened to the words. Justin's gaze told me he meant each and every one of them.

TWO

JUSTIN

"Your Body Is A Wonderland" played in our sea-view room. John Mayer's smooth voice blended with the sweet sounds coming from Sarah's mouth. I covered her lips with mine, swallowing her moan as I shifted inside her, grinding deeper until she tore her lips from me and let out a smile-inducing cry.

"You feel so good," she groaned, gripping my ass cheeks and driving me even deeper.

I buried my face in her hair and thrust into her, our naked skin slapping together as the pressure built inside me. Our sizzling energy grew, contrasting with the mellow song, until we were moaning in unison. The heady friction increased to a blinding explosion. I held her to me and shuddered, my cry muffled in the crook of her neck as I emptied myself inside her.

Rising onto my elbows, I gazed down at her gorgeous face. She was shining. She had been our entire honeymoon, and I hoped to keep that look on her face for the rest of my life. With a giggle, she reached for the remote and rewound our *honeymoon song*. John Mayer's guitar riff started up again as I rolled off her and rested my head on my arm. Starting at her belly button, I traced a soft line up her body, rounding both breasts before tracking up to her collarbone. She closed her eyes with a wistful sigh as the ocean breeze ruffled the net curtains covering the open window.

"This is perfection." She ran her small fingers up my arm, her face the picture of tranquil beauty.

We only had four days of our honeymoon left. Tomorrow, Blake and Jane were arriving, and we'd be caught up in a whirlwind of wedding prep. The last ten days had been nothing but perfect. Since meeting each other four years earlier, we'd never spent this much time alone. After we got engaged, we moved in with Blake and Jane. I loved living with my brother and his girl, but having Sarah all to myself had been everything I didn't realize I'd been craving.

Mr. Torrence's offer of his house in LA didn't seem like such a bad idea anymore. When he'd first suggested it, Sarah had jumped up and hugged him so fast, I hadn't even had time to think about it before agreeing. Living in a place owned by my in-laws wasn't exactly the start I wanted. Especially since my father-in-law scared the living crap out of me. But Sarah had been so touched, and encouraged, by his offer that I couldn't refuse her sparkling eyes. Blake told me it'd be okay and it was a great way to really get ourselves set up.

"You're not going to find rent that sweet anywhere else, lil' bro. Go for it."

Blake had a point. It was an easy start to the marriage. We could save more money and start putting aside some funds so Sarah would be able to set up her own business one day. She had big dreams but still wasn't sure she could make them come true. I was going to prove her wrong.

My finger crested Sarah's chin. I traced a line around her soft lips and over her nose before splaying my hand across her cheek and pulling her close to me. She nestled against my chest. It was her turn to draw now. Her finger wove around my chest, a soft tickle that would soon lead to more.

A smile pushed my lips wide. I wasn't going to complain about spending the entire day making love to my wife.

*****

I stood behind my brother, snickering at him while he straightened his chocolate brown bowtie for the tenth time in fifteen minutes.

"D-dude, would you s-stop. You look great."

"I know." Blake shook out his shoulders before running a hand over his head. His wild curls had been tamed into a stubby ponytail that looked like a rabbit's tail at the nape of his neck.

He did look great. In true Sarah style, she'd taken into account looks and personality. Blake and Jane's wedding was completely different from ours.

We went for smooth lines and minimalism.

Blake and Jane were the opposite. Unlike my black tux, Blake wore a chocolate brown suit with cream pinstripe. Blake hadn't seen it yet, but his wife was in a stunning dress—the top half a fitted bodice covered in hand-cut leaves. Sarah had painstakingly made each and every one, creating a mix of orange, red, and yellow awesomeness. In spite of the fact this was a summer wedding, Sarah and Jane had decided on an autumn theme. When I suggested they wait and actually get married in the fall, they both balked at me like I was crazy.

"I've waited long enough to marry your brother, thank you very much." Jane's pointed look shut me up, and so my big bro was having a cross-season wedding.

He looked down at his pointy brown shoes, tapping the heels together and admitting, "I can't believe how nervous I am."

I frowned. "Neither can I. It's normally y-you who has your shit t-together."

"It's my wedding day, man. Gimme a break."

My smile was broad, no doubt showing off the dimple on my left cheek. "It's Jane. Forget about everything else and focus on that one fact."

Blake's chest puffed out at my words, his eyes flickering with a spark of joy I knew only too well. "Will you go and check on her for me?"

"What? Now?"

"Yeah, you take the car and I'll bring the bike in a few. Just pop your head in and see how she's doing. If she's as nervous as me, she'll appreciate a check-in."

"Sarah and the girls are with her, man. S-she's gonna be f-fine."

"I know. I just..." Blake shrugged. "Do you mind?"

I had to hesitate. As best man, I kind of felt like it was my duty to stay with my brother and make sure he got to the church on time. Breaking with tradition, Blake and Jane had only opted for a small wedding party. I was the only groomsmen. Was it really right to leave my brother on such a crucial day in his life?

But Sarah was at the church. She'd be with Jane, helping her get ready. I'd been forced to spend the night without her, and I was already aching. I'd be able to see her for a few minutes before the service, maybe steal a kiss or two.

So, in spite of the fact it was kind of selfish, I patted my brother on the arm and smiled. "Of course I don't mind."

Blake threw me the keys, and after a quick selfie to cement the moment, I headed out to the car, my shiny shoes scuffing on the uneven concrete. I stopped to give them a quick rub. Sarah had spent hours perfecting the look of this wedding; I wasn't going to let her down with marks on my shoes.

Spending the night without her had been awful. Not only were we in separate beds, but separate hotels as well. Jane had wanted a girly night painting her nails and stuff, and Blake and I did the boys' night out. We'd gone to a local pub with Jane's dad and ours, played darts, listened to an indie rock band, and gotten back to our room by eleven. It was hardly wild, but it'd been exactly what Blake was after. Getting married had brought out a maturity in him I'd never seen before. He was taking the commitment seriously and vowed to be the best husband he could to Jane. Which meant no crazy antics the night before the wedding.

I told him he'd never be as good a husband as I was going to be to Sarah.

He slapped his glass down and grinned. "Bring it on, buddy."

It was a good challenge to give each other, and I couldn't wait to live up to my end of it.

THREE

SARAH

Jane giggled as I fluffed around with her hair. She looked radiant in the autumn dress I'd designed. The colorful leaves matched her red hair, the tones making her pale, Irish complexion rosy. I swept her long bangs to the side, pinning them back before reaching for the veil.

"I feel so beautiful." Her mild English accent had grown stronger with her return home. She'd been living in the United States for several years, but she'd spent most of her childhood in England. They moved to the States when her father's job at the American Embassy came to an end, so the poor girl had been made to transfer countries and high schools at the age of fifteen.

I stood back from her, patting her shoulders with a smirk. "That's because you are beautiful."

"Not normally *this* beautiful."

"Blake's going to go crazy when he sees you."

Jane let out a nervous giggle, her pinky finger trembling as she wiped it below her eye. I had to admit that my friend had been a bit of a stress-bucket leading up to her big day. She was no bridezilla, but she found it really hard to step back. Thankfully, she was my best friend and I adored her, so it wasn't hard having her hover over each and every aspect. She'd liked most of my ideas, which helped. But the last few days, she'd been borderline cray-cray. The girl needed to get the day over with so she could relax. I was glad they decided to take their honeymoon straight after the wedding. Like us, they'd planned a two-week affair that would have them fully rejuvenated before returning to work.

Fitting the veil in place, I walked behind her so I could adjust it properly. The cream tulle was light, and framed her face perfectly. I tweaked the edge then stepped back and assessed her in the mirror.

"You look so pwetty, Geowjana." Florence, the little flower girl, tipped back in her ballet slippers, sounding adorable as she tried to pronounce Jane's full name—Georjana. I grinned at the way her strawberry-blonde ringlets bounced when she danced over to us.

Standing beside her towering cousin, she looked

in the mirror and giggled, swishing from side to side in her adorable empire line dress with the autumn leaves sprinkling down the skirt. It was easy to see she felt like a princess.

"You both look amazing." I shook my head with a dreamy smile, picturing Blake's gaze as his future bride walked down the aisle toward him. The day was going to be magical. *Not quite as magical as mine, of course.* I internally giggled at the thought, my body aching for a taste of my husband. The previous night without him had been horrible. I was surprised by just how much I missed him. Having spent the past two weeks doing everything with him, it was a cold shock to endure a night alone.

I couldn't wait until after the reception, when I could take him back to our room and rip all his clothes off. A hot blush burned my cheeks. I shifted behind Jane's tall body so she couldn't see me in the mirror. Thankfully, she was engrossed in an animated discussion with Florence, so both of them were oblivious that my mind was racing with images of Justin's naked body thrusting against mine. The thoughts were so tantalizing and strong I could feel heat pooling between my legs. I had to question the chances of me lasting until after the reception. Maybe I could pull him into a darkened room while everyone was dancing…you know, a little quickie to get us in the mood for the rest of our night.

I wasn't usually a sex fiend, but Justin brought out the naughty in me. Any time, any place with that man.

A light knock on the door had me biting my grin and reining in my thoughts.

"Come in," I called while Jane leaned toward the mirror to quadruple-check her makeup.

The door creaked open, and I glanced back in time to see Justin's gorgeous face. My heart skipped then took off running when he smiled at me.

"What are you doing here?" Jane squeaked. "Is everything okay?"

Justin chuckled. "Everything's fine. B-Blake just wanted me to come and check on his bride."

She let out a swooning sigh and patted her chest. "I love that man."

I giggled and stepped back, adjusting the veil one last time. I lifted it high then let it drop. The fabric floated down then nestled into place, just the way I designed it to.

Florence started up again about how beautiful Jane looked. I caught Justin's eye and grinned when he mouthed, "You're gorgeous."

I flashed him a look that hopefully gave away how hot I was. He picked up on it immediately, because his forehead dipped while his eyes sparked with hunger. I brushed my tongue over my lower lip, following it with a light scraping of my teeth.

The heat in Justin's gaze intensified.

"I'll be back in a sec." I patted Jane's shoulder. She was too distracted giggling with her little cousin to notice me slipping out of the room.

As soon as the door was shut, Justin pulled me into his arms, kissing me like we'd been apart for months. I swirled my tongue around his, gripping the back of his neck and pressing my body against him.

"Come on," I whispered against his lips, before tugging his wrist and hustling us to the room at the end of the hallway. I'd found the dimly lit office the day before when I was decorating the church. It was sparsely furnished with one wooden desk and a round-backed chair that looked uncomfortable to sit in. Against the wall was a rickety bookshelf with volumes of hardback books that could no doubt bore me to tears.

I glanced away from the dusty manuals and slipped off my underwear. Justin's eyes bulged, but he didn't protest as I hiked up my silk dress and perched my bare butt on the edge of the desk. I made sure the fabric was well clear before spreading my legs and tugging Justin toward me. He crushed his mouth to mine as I started unbuttoning his pants.

"I missed you," he murmured between kisses. "I couldn't stop thinking about you last night."

I guided his hand between my thighs as he ran his tongue down my neck. The urgency firing between us was insane.

He pushed his fingers inside me, igniting rockets of pleasure. I was so hot for him already it wouldn't take much for me to come. "You're already wet," he puffed against my mouth.

"You're already hard," I countered with a

giggle, pulling down his pants and wrapping my fingers around his erection.

He groaned into my mouth and I giggled again, squeezing a little harder and sliding my finger over his moist head. He felt so damn good.

"I need you inside me," I whispered.

Tucking his hand beneath my knee, he lifted my leg and positioned himself at my entrance. He made me wait a whole beat before sliding into me. I couldn't hold back my lusty cry but he captured it with his hot mouth, lashing his tongue against mine as he thrust into me.

The passion between us was scorching and had an animalistic quality that couldn't be quenched fast enough.

I clenched his erection, drawing him in. I couldn't get enough of his power. He drove into me, and I had to bite my lips together to stop myself from crying out again. People would be filling the church already. Getting busted spread eagle on a minister's office desk with my husband's pants around his ankles would not go down well. I could just imagine my father-in-law's reaction.

A nervous giggle rose inside me, but Justin's thrusting cut it short. He was hitting all the right spots, making it impossible not to whimper just a little.

I clung to his shoulders, puffing against his jacket as he pumped hard and fast. My head fell back and I bit my lower lip as Justin dragged my butt even closer. I leaned back on the desk, bracing myself on shaky arms while he picked up the pace.

I let out a mewling cry as the pressure inside me mounted like a rumbling volcano. He gripped my ass and drove even harder until a heated explosion rocketed through both of us. I couldn't hold back my cry. Justin pressed his hand over my mouth, laughing as he pulled me back against him. His arms were quivering a little, and as I laid my head against his chest, I could hear his thundering heartbeat.

My heart matched his. I'm sure it had never raced so fast before. Justin looked down at me with glazed eyes, a slow, drunken smile tugging at his lips.

"That was hot," I puffed. "We have to do that again. The risk of getting caught totally does it for me."

His eyes gleamed with promise, and I couldn't help a giddy titter.

He claimed my mouth, slow and easy, before pulling away from me. I felt the loss keenly, but knowing I'd get it again in a few hours helped soften the blow. Justin helped me clean up, even kneeling on the floor and holding out my underwear so I could step back into it. He pulled my panties into place then trailed his fingers down my thighs, his smile wicked and playful.

I bit my lip then whispered, "You keep looking at me like that, and I won't be able to resist an immediate second round."

He cleared his throat, a bright blush warming his cheeks as he stood tall and arranged my layers of silky fabric. All evidence of our tryst was hopefully hidden away as we walked out of the room with innocent expressions. Okay, maybe not so innocent. It was kind of hard to hide our smiles.

We stopped outside Jane's dressing room and kissed one more time. Justin blessed me with another dreamy smile then whispered, "I'll see you soon."

He brushed his lips across my nose then sauntered away. I watched him until he'd disappeared around the corner, then floated into Jane's dressing room. This would be the second time in two weeks that I'd be walking down the aisle toward him. It looked like I'd be in for another day of constant smiles and loved-up insides. Weddings were the best.

FOUR

JUSTIN

I walked back out to the main entrance of the stone church. It was impossible not to step with a slight bounce. My wife was freaking hot. I loved her passion, her energy, the fire she could light within me. I was certain we'd never be able to get enough of each other. Making love to Sarah was like nothing else on this planet. Being married to her topped everything.

I didn't even bother hiding my grin when I stopped to look down the aisle. We'd spent the day before decorating it with orange and yellow roses, plus these lilies—calla something or other. They looked amazing. Bringing Sarah's vision to life was inspiring. To say I was proud of my wife's creative talent was an understatement. The woman was an artistic genius. She'd turned the little stone chapel into a magical realm with fairy lights, frost cloth, and vines. Combined with the splash of autumn colors and the aromatic scent of roses, the place was enchanting.

Watching Sarah walk down the aisle in her silky dress was going to be nothing but a pleasure. I scanned the pews, noting a few familiar faces before turning to look out the open double doors. People were walking down the pathway, dressed in their finery. Age was reflected in fashion choices, from the chic party dresses and stiletto heels to the muted pastel outfits and hats with flowers in them. Plucking out my phone, I snapped a few quick shots then took a twenty-second video, scanning over the decorated archway then back outside. The footage would be great for the wedding montage video I was making Blake and Jane. That was my thing. I loved putting together short clips to music. Still shots and live footage would be intermingled to create a four-minute piece of magic. I absolutely loved sitting at my computer and putting them together…and I loved people's reactions even more. They made for perfect gifts.

I tucked my phone away as Dad appeared. He was in his standard wedding tux, looking stately and every bit the college professor he was. My insides kicked with instant warning like they always did. I didn't know what it was about the guy, but he put me on edge without even trying. We'd never said as much to each other, but it was obvious Blake was his favorite and I was the one who never quite cut it.

"H-hey, Dad." I smiled.

"What are you doing here?" His dark eyebrows met in the middle when he frowned at me.

I cleared my throat and smoothed down my brown jacket. "Blake asked me t-to come early and ch-check in on J-J-J..." I gave up. He knew who I was talking about.

Dad tried to hide his disappointment behind a smile. My stutter had always bothered him. Ironically, I stuttered more around him than anyone.

He patted me on the shoulder with a closed-mouth smile. "My two boys. After today, you'll both be married men. You and Blake chose well."

I nodded, appreciating the compliment.

"He sh-should be here any minute. He's..." My voice stopped for a second, like it sometimes did. Imagine a fist blocking your windpipe while your brain struggles to punch out the word. It was like that. I closed my eyes and pictured myself talking to Sarah. "He's coming on the bike." The words eased out my mouth like running water.

"Okay, son. Why don't you go say hi to your mother then find your place upfront. I'll keep an eye out for him."

Unwilling to risk stuttering again, I bobbed my head and set off down the aisle. Mom greeted me with a kiss and told me I looked handsome. I then rehashed the same conversation I'd just had with Dad before Mom patted me on the cheek and sent me up the two steps to wait for my brother.

I had to admit what an honor it was to be the only groomsman. Blake was one of those guys with hundreds of friends. Everyone was Blake's buddy, but he reserved the best friend role for me. Jane didn't want a large wedding, especially with having it overseas, so the couple opted for just me and Sarah to accompany them. Suited me just fine.

Checking my watch, I noted the time. There was only ten minutes until the ceremony started. It surprised me that Blake hadn't turned up already. We'd been raised to be on time...and it was his wedding. The guy must have been more nervous than I thought.

Resting my hand on top of my watch, I tapped the glass with my finger and tried to look casual while I waited. People continued to filter into the church. I smiled at the various guests, recognizing most of them from the engagement party. The small chapel was abuzz with the quiet murmur of excited guests as they marveled and pointed at the stunning decor. If my chest puffed with any more pride, my shirt would pop open.

I couldn't wait for Sarah to walk down the aisle toward me again. Seeing her do that on our wedding day nearly had me in tears. I managed to keep up my calm exterior, but my insides had been a wreck...and soon it would be Blake's turn.

A grin pushed at my cheeks as I imagined watching my brother go through it all. I was so stoked to be a part of it.

Movement at the back of the church caught my eye. I craned my neck, expecting to see Blake sauntering down the aisle with a confident, relaxed smile in place. But it was just my dad chatting with some guests. I checked my watch again and frowned.

Since when was a groom late to his wedding? Usually it was some bridal emergency, but I'd checked in on Jane and she was ready. Shit, I should have called to let him know. I got distracted with Sarah…and then Dad. I pulled out my phone and called Blake.

No one answered.

My gut probably should have started clenching at that point, but the idea of something bad happening to my brother on his wedding day was so left field that it hadn't even occurred to me.

I figured he was probably taking a minute to gather himself. If he didn't show up in ten minutes, I'd take the car to collect him.

Mom gripped the shiny red clutch in her lap. She was chatting with my aunt in the row behind her, but the tense set of her shoulders gave away how unimpressed she was. Blake never did much to upset my parents, but being late on his wedding day? I snickered and shook my head while checking my phone again.

Still nothing.

I unlocked the screen and redialed my brother, but I hung up before the call went through. Something at the back of the church made my heart spasm.

"Dad?" I rushed down the steps and ran up the aisle, ready to catch my father. He stumbled against one of the wooden pews, his eyes wild as he clutched the phone to his chest.

I reached out my arm to steady him and he gripped my jacket, his face twisting with agony. I thought he was having a heart attack or something.

"Dad! What is it?"

"Blake," he whispered, his face a mask of anguish.

I'd never been shot before, but that look in my father's eyes…the way he whispered my brother's name. It killed me.

He didn't have to say anything else. I felt it in my soul.

Blake was gone.

I didn't know how it happened. All my brain could scream in that moment was that my brother was dead.

FIVE

SARAH

The smell of dirt was pungent, wafting up my nostrils and making me sick. But it was the only thing I could focus on. The rest of my body was numb. I didn't want to see the coffin being lowered in the ground, or watch Jane's face crumple as her puffy red eyes filled with even more tears. Her parents flanked her, holding her up as she watched her college sweetheart finally laid to rest.

Justin stood beside me, so silent and still he could have been mistaken for a statue. He hadn't spoken much since returning from the crash site. All I'd managed to get out of him was that Blake had died on impact, so at least he hadn't suffered. I'd learned later from his father that the police thought Blake must have been driving on the wrong side of the road. As an American, he was used to driving on the right. He must have had a slight lapse in concentration and shifted into the opposite lane, easy enough to do on the winding country road. The car coming toward him had been speeding. With no helmet, Blake hadn't stood a chance. Apparently, the woman driving the car had died at the scene. I knew nothing about her, but if she'd come from a family like Blake's, her death would have caused multiple heartache.

I scanned the crowd surrounding Blake's plot. Everyone wore black. It felt weird, because Blake was such a colorful guy. It seemed right that we should be in bright yellows and flashy reds, but this funeral echoed a deep mourning rather than a celebration of life. Blake was taken too soon, his sudden death tragic and debilitating. I had no idea how Jane would go on with her life. To lose her fiancé on their wedding day. It was a sick joke.

Shuffling closer to Justin, I looked up at his blank expression, my heart squeezing with fear. How was he going to continue? Blake had always been his rock, his best friend. They were only a year apart in age, practically twins. Justin hadn't said as much, but surely he must have felt like half of him was missing.

Jane's sob cut through the gray skies. Covering her mouth, she bent over while her father clutched her to his side, trying to support her weight.

Tendrils of red hair framed her pale face, her green eyes haunting as the minister finished his prayer. Clutching the yellow rose to her chest, she stumbled forward, her body quaking as she kissed the petals then dropped it into the hole.

Tears flooded my eyes. I sucked in a shaky breath then let it out on a whimper as we were encouraged to follow suit. Painful minutes ticked by as we each shuffled forward and dropped our roses—yellow memories of a guy who had touched and blessed us all in different ways.

Justin's limbs acted like wood. He gripped the rose stem, unable to let go until I gently pried his fingers loose. He stared down at me, his grief-stricken gaze working like a torment. What was going through his mind? Would he ever talk to me again?

Had Jane and I both lost our husbands on her wedding day?

*****

I rubbed the moisturizer into my hands while I stared at Justin in the mirror. He was lying on the bed, gazing up at the ceiling with the concrete expression he'd had in place all day.

We were spending the night in his childhood bedroom in Albuquerque. I'd never been in the house without Blake and Jane. It seemed cold and quiet without them. Jane and her parents had returned to LA that night. For the sake of Justin's parents, we decided to stay until the day before we were due at work. I couldn't believe our new life was beginning so soon. It seemed ridiculous. Life had been thrown on its head, yet the world kept on turning. People kept waking up each morning and going about their day as if one of the best people on the planet hadn't been killed.

Soft music played from the stereo next to Justin's pillow. I couldn't remember putting it on, but I appreciated it. Justin's silence was suffocating. I wished he'd let me in, but he'd always been the kind to take his time.

Flicking off the main light, I straightened my pajama shirt before crawling into bed with my husband. His eyes were locked on the ceiling, his hands threaded on his chest.

"Justin," I whispered.

But he wouldn't look at me.

He just muttered, "Yeah?"

And I couldn't think of anything to say.

A fresh song started on the radio, "Rough Water" by Travie McCoy. Jason Mraz sang the first few lines and my soul kicked in, wrapping around the lyrics and wanting to make them mine. Reaching for Justin's wrist, I pulled his arm wide and found my place against him.

Normally, his arms would encircle me, dragging me as close as possible, but that night they were floppy and unresponsive.

"Justin," I whispered again, my voice hitching as desperation fired through me. "Please, hold me."

His body stiffened as I nestled my head into the crook of his neck.

"Don't let me go. Please, don't let me drown. We need each other right now."

His muscles beneath my chin were taut and reticent, but I clutched his side and kept going.

"I'm claiming this song for us. I'm holding you for as long as it takes. I won't let you drown."

A long, slow breath oozed out of him, his body finally responding. I closed my eyes, tears scorching me as his arm wound around my back and pulled me to his side. I tucked my knee over his thigh and sniffled into his chest.

"Promise me?" My voice trembled. "Promise you won't let me go."

"Never." His voice was hoarse and deep as he gripped me tighter. "I'll never let you go."

Relieved tears trickled out the corners of my eyes, renewed hope fluttering inside me. Everything was shit right now, but we'd make it. We'd survive, as long as we kept holding on to each other.

SIX

JUSTIN

The first day of work at Torrence Records, I didn't know how I was supposed to feel. My guess was a mixture of nerves and excitement. My reality was a sick, toxic bile that swirled in my stomach. I didn't want to be there.

"Justin Doyle, welcome." Everett Torrence's smile was broad and a little tight. I didn't miss the slight narrowing of his eyes as he assessed me. I was a short, puny man beside him. Trying not to let that show, I forced my shoulders back and looked him in the eye.

"Th-thank you, s-sir."

Everett nodded then moved aside so Clay, the lawyer who'd be mentoring me, could shake my hand as well.

"Nice to see you again," he said with a grin.

I had to conjure a smile. It was an effort. I hadn't smiled much since the worst day of my life. Images of Blake's lifeless gaze taunted me. I stiffened to counter the shudder that tore through my body every time I relived that moment. Guilt ate at me, taking out huge chunks of my insides.

I should have been there for him. I should have been driving that narrow winding road while he sweated beside me in a car with airbags and a seatbelt to protect him. Instead, I'd left him with a motorbike so I could go screw my wife on a dusty office desk. While I was coming inside her, he was bleeding out in a ditch.

"So, this is the floor you'll be working on." Clay stepped out of the elevator and led me to the reception desk. A lady with dark brown curls and an open smile greeted me.

"I'm Marcia." She held out her hand and I shook it while a guy with scruffy hair and a playful grin approached me.

"Marcus Chapman." He shook my hand. His grip was firm yet friendly. "If you need anything, don't hesitate to ask."

"Thanks." I nodded, forcing yet another smile. My face was going to hurt by the end of the day.

As I walked down the corridor and met a hundred other people, my mind wandered to Sarah. I wondered how she was getting on with her first day. She'd been nervous and jittery as we got ready. The skirt and blouse she'd chosen made her look like a supermodel, and I'd stolen glances of her curvaceous frame as she wiggled into her outfit. She'd kept her blonde waves loose and free, and I fought the urge to run my fingers through them when I kissed her good-bye.

I wanted her so bad, but I hadn't been able to bring myself to make love to her once since Blake's death. Guilt had wrapped me up so tight I wasn't sure I'd ever break free of it. She was so beautiful, so deserving…and I was just the useless man who let his best friend die.

I didn't know how I'd ever get back to the man she deserved. People always said time healed things. I guess I just had to rely on that.

"And this is your office." I stepped into the small space, my eyes trailing over the shiny black desk. A laptop stand with a new keyboard beneath it took up the right side. On the shelves behind were stacks of law books that I'd had sent over when I moved to LA. My stomach twisted into tight knots as I imagined diving into them. Studying for a law degree was the last thing I felt like doing, but my parents had been so hopeful when I graduated.

"And the family tradition continues. You and Blake following in my footsteps couldn't make me prouder." Mom's merry laughter had felt like a cheese grater on my skull at the time, but I'd smiled and nodded like the good son I was.

I looked at Clay. "Th-this looks great. Th-

43

thanks."

"No problem. I'll let you get settled in. Tech will pop in shortly to help you set up emails, et cetera. If we could meet in an hour, I'd like to debrief you on the week and go over the jobs I'd like to get started with."

"S-sounds good." My voice was distant and wooden, but Clay didn't seem to notice.

He bustled out of the room, his gait fast and purposeful. With a heavy sigh, I shuffled around to my new office chair. It smelled leathery and had a brand-new feel about it. The wheels slid smoothly as I pulled it out then slumped into it.

Taking out my laptop, I placed it on my near-empty desk and looked around the office. Still no nerves or excitement...just a stormy bile that surged within, like a foul-smelling squall threatening to drown me.

Lifting the lid, I sought solace in the only thing to ease my discomfort. Double-clicking my movie folder, I brought up a clip of Sarah. I'd given it to her the night we celebrated our *year since meeting* anniversary. The backing track was "I See You" by Mika. He was an artist Jane introduced me to, and that song in particular would be burned into my memory forever. It was playing when I met Sarah. I would never forget the way I felt when I glanced across Jane's sorority house party and spotted her for the first time. Everything else around me faded—Blake drinking beer beside me, people laughing and dancing on the floor. There was only this beautiful woman. She was exquisite. A smile that could guide ships into a harbor…eyes that could stand in for the stars. She stood in the center of the room, slowly swaying to the beat. Her slender arms swished from side to side, like she was dancing in water.

Blake snickered beside me, then I got nudged in the arm so hard the beer nearly slipped from my hand.

"Okay, which girl are you gaping at? It better not be mine."

I shook my head. "Who is that?"

Blake leaned closer to me, trying to see who I was staring at. "The blonde?"

"The o-one with the s-sp-sp-sparkles."

My brother gave me a weird look. "Which one?"

Jane appeared beside us, wrapping her arm around Blake. "Hey, sexy."

He grinned and pulled her closer, kissing her forehead.

"Who are we looking at?" She rose to her tiptoes and followed my line of sight.

"G-girl." I was pathetic. But the girl was seriously way too beautiful for words.

Jane giggled and looked at Blake. My brother shrugged. "Something about sparkles."

His girlfriend looked again then started nodding. "Oh, you mean Sarah."

"Sarah." The word whispered out of my mouth, tasting sweet.

"Yeah, she's a freshman too. Just became a sister last week. You should go talk to her."

I sucked in a breath and shook my head.

"Oh, come on." Jane squeezed my forearm. "You'll be great."

"I-I can't t-talk to her. I-I'll make a f-f-f..." I closed my eyes and pressed my lips together before punching out the word. "Fool of myself."

Jane's smile was sympathetic, but Blake never let me get away with using my stutter as an excuse for anything.

"Don't be an idiot. The chances of you blowing her away with your charm and intelligence are much higher. Go for it, man."

I shot him a skeptical frown, but he just grabbed the bottle from my hand and nudged me into the room. I took two steps before jerking to a stop. Sarah turned my way, her eyes landing straight on me. She assessed me for a moment before her pale pink lips rose with a smile.

The song continued to pump through me. The words "But I see you" tugged at my hesitation, urging me forward. But it wasn't until Jane grabbed my wrist and yanked me through the partygoers that I found myself face to face with the most beautiful creature I'd ever seen.

"Sarah," Jane said, "I'd like you to meet my boyfriend's brother, Justin."

Her eyes sparkled and she stuck out her hand. "Hi, Justin."

What a voice. It was sweet and pure, like cotton candy at a country fair.

"Hi." I wrapped my fingers around hers and something inside me shifted. A warmth I didn't recognize swirled through me, and a bright smile stretched my cheeks wide. "So, Jane tells me this is your

46

first year at Stanford. Mine too."

"Oh, really? Isn't it so terrifying? I mean, exciting, but also just…overwhelming."

I nodded, my dreamy smile no doubt looking stupid.

She didn't seem to notice.

"So, what are you studying?" She tucked a lock of hair behind her ear, and I answered her…and then she answered my question, and before I knew it, we were sitting in the corner of the living room immersed in a conversation so deep and enthralling the outside world became nothing more than blurry shadows.

I didn't kiss her that night, but I asked her if she wanted to study with me in the library. She agreed and I floated back to my dorm room at four o'clock in the morning.

It wasn't until my head touched the pillow that I realized something mind-blowing.

I'd spent my night hanging out with God's most beautiful creation…and I hadn't stuttered once.

I clicked on the clip and watched Sarah—her eyes, her sparkle. She grinned at the camera in a thousand different ways. My gaze grew fuzzy as I stared at the screen. The heavy bleakness I couldn't shake surrounded me like a damp fog.

Would I ever see her smile like that again? So unchecked and carefree?

The last week had been filled with nothing but tears and heartache. Things that could have so easily been prevented.

Seeing her pale face and puffy eyes morph with pain like that, I didn't know what to do. She made me promise to hold her, and I would. But how could I keep her afloat when I felt like I was drowning?

Jane... my parents. Their pain felt like knives plunging into me. I'd let them all down. I'd ruined everything.

Slapping my laptop closed, I pushed away and spun to snatch a law book off the shelf. Thumping it onto the desk, I flipped it open to the first mind-numbing chapter.

I had to make up for my mistake.

I had to work my ass off. Blake had always been the better man. It should have been me in that ditch, not him. Somehow, I had to rise above my pain and be the person they needed me to be.

I'd make my parents proud. I'd win over Sarah's father. I'd provide for her. I'd earn, I'd save, I'd work. She deserved a good life, and I had to somehow give that to her.

I had to prove myself worthy of life.

I would never be as amazing as Blake, but I would give everything to become the person people wanted me to be.

SEVEN

SARAH

Eleven months later...

"You're killing me." Maria laughed, slapping the table and making her cutlery dance.

My smile was tight as I watched her eyes bulge. She was pointing to our mother and shaking her head.

"Tell me that's not true." My eldest sister, Libby, leaned forward. "That's so unfair! Daddy's taking you to Bora Bora? It's not even an important anniversary. It's like, what? Thirty-three years.

That's not one of the significant numbers."

Mom shrugged, trying to play down her growing smile. "What can I say, your father likes to celebrate."

"Ugh." Maria rolled her eyes but gave me a little wink as she raised the wine glass to her lips.

"The last time Trent did anything romantic for me was before Brayden was born," Libby muttered.

Maria gasped. "That's like ten years ago. Please tell me you guys still have sex."

Libby grinned. "We have three children, of course we have sex."

"Okay, rephrase." Maria pointed her finger in the air. "Please tell me you guys have had sex more than three times."

The table shifted as Libby tried to kick our sister. Maria squawked and swung her legs out of the way.

"Shh, girls." Mom's soft reprimand was ignored as my sisters laughed at each other. We were in a classy little restaurant with white tablecloths and bulbous wineglasses. One did not kick another under the table in such places.

"Of course we have sex. If anything, it's gotten better with time." Libby gave us an imperious smirk as she reached for her wineglass.

I swallowed, not saying anything as Maria perked up. "That's good to know, because seriously, having twin boys has murdered my sex life. We used to do it all the time, now we're just too tired. Children suck the life out of you."

Maria turned to me, clutching my arm. "Don't

rush into babies, Sparky. You enjoy your man while you can."

Mom cleared her throat, her cheeks heating with color as she patted her daughter's arm. "Maria, your boys are only two. You will get your sanity…and your sex life back, believe me." She winked and smiled at us while we each made slightly awkward faces at her. She tipped her hands with an exasperated sigh. "Oh, so I have to sit here listening to your sex lives, but I'm not allowed to subtly refer to the fact your father's a stallion in the bedroom."

"Ewww, Mom!" We all groaned in unison while she snickered, triumphantly flicking back her short hair and sitting up straighter.

My stomach revolted against a flood of images swarming me. I tried to counter them with memories of Justin and me in the bedroom. Picturing my sexy man buried inside me was hot and could definitely burn Mom's mean tidbit from my mind.

But there was just one little—*major*—problem.

I couldn't remember the last time we'd had sex.

Since returning from England and Jane's nightmare wedding day, I could count on one hand the number of times we'd slept together. Life had swallowed us whole. Work took over, dragging me into a world of fashion that I loved. But the hours were really long. And I wasn't the only one working my ass off. Some days, Justin and I barely saw each other. I'd fall into bed after he'd gone to sleep, and then he'd be up and out the door before

I'd woken in the morning.

When the hell were we supposed to fit sex into the equation?

Holidays were taken up with family time...and that wasn't exactly the happiest of occasions. The Doyle family Christmas in New Mexico had been a solemn, empty affair. Blake's absence was like a freaking black hole, but no one wanted to talk about it.

And the weekends were filled with Justin studying for his law degree and me immersed in my sketchbook—my sanctuary.

I took a sip from my wineglass, holding the liquid in my mouth before pushing it down my thick throat.

"Sarah, you're quiet today, sweetie." Mom smiled at me while reaching for her own glass.

I snickered and shrugged as I tried to brush off the three curious gazes.

Maria rolled her eyes. "She's probably thinking about the hot ass she's going to get tonight."

"Maria," Mom chided.

"Oh, come on, Mom." Libby giggled. "First year of marriage." She let out a dreamy sigh and looked to the ceiling. "You couldn't get Trent and me out of the bedroom some weekends."

I forced a laugh, my cheeks burning with color.

"Oh, there it is." Maria pointed at me. "Look at that face. You and Justin are like bunny rabbits, aren't you?"

"I think it's about time I head back to work." I made sure my voice was light and bouncy, not wanting to give away my thundering heartbeat or the way my stomach curdled at the truth screaming through my brain.

"Oh, no, you don't. You've got ten minutes left." Maria tapped her watch.

Our lunch dates were a monthly thing my mother insisted on. I didn't mind so much, but some days I felt like my sister in New York, Annabelle, was the lucky one. Usually, we spoke about stuff like kids and houses and education. Safe topics. If I'd known that particular lunch was going to be a sex-ed on my family's marriages, I would have given it a miss.

Before I strutted my busy butt into the restaurant, I would have told anyone that my marriage was doing okay. We were a busy, professional couple, working hard so we could eventually achieve our goals.

But watching Libby's face as she talked about her first year of marriage, and the way Mom's eyes danced as she talked about Dad? I couldn't imagine Justin and me ever getting to that point. Not the rate we were going.

And our goals?

What goals?

I couldn't even remember what they were.

We were both just busy trying to survive.

Forcing my lips into a smile, I tried to hide my thoughts. Mom told Dad everything, and I didn't need to give my father any kind of fuel against Justin. If he thought I was even the tiniest bit unhappy, he'd find a way to blame my husband.

Having a protective father came with some serious downsides.

My unhappiness wasn't all Justin's fault.

Work was my haven, where nothing bad could touch me.

It was easier being there than facing the silent agony of home. Blake's death had done something to us, something I couldn't even identify. It was too hard, too big to talk about. So I hid out at work…and Justin did the same.

I winked at Maria then looked at my mother. "Congratulations on the upcoming wedding anniversary, Mom. I hope your holiday is amazing. You deserve it."

"Thank you, sweet girl." She gave me her *I love you so much* smile, and I grinned back, reaching across the table and giving her hand a squeeze.

"Sorry, but I really have to go. Enjoy the rest of your lunch, ladies."

"Enjoy your sex tonight." Maria sang the last word, making Libby giggle.

I punched out a laugh and swatted her arm. "Behave, you."

She slapped me on the butt as I walked away from the table. I gave it a wiggle, putting on the show they wanted. I was the playful younger sister, the sweet girl with the ready smile. They didn't need to know about my limp heart and the fact it started gasping for air every time I walked through my front door.

Clearing my throat, I lifted my chin and shook the thought from my mind. Powering back to work, I strode into the office, determined to disappear into layers of fabric and joy. I set down my handbag and smiled at Jules. He had a pencil between his teeth, so he settled for wiggling his eyebrows at me.

I chuckled and pulled out my stool, ready to sit.

"Sarah, Enrique would like to see you in his office." Chantelle brushed past my work table, her demure smile barely moving her cheeks.

"Okay." I followed after her, flicking a glance over my shoulder. Jules was giving me a big thumbs-up and shaking his hips in a happy dance.

I bit back my smile and tried to quell the anxious giggles rocking my stomach. Readjusting my loose, powder blue shirt with the black polka dots, I made sure it sat just right before smoothing my hands down my fitted ankle-length pants and nervously walking into Enrique DeMarco's office.

The man was a celebrity in the fashion industry. What his parents had started, and he had grown, was amazing. I'd always loved Echelon Fashion's designs, and being offered a job there still blew my mind sometimes. I couldn't believe it. Fresh out of college and working for one of the most prestigious fashion houses in the industry. It was insane.

Enrique sat behind his desk, looking suave in his charcoal business suit. The man oozed a cool kind of charm that most guys could only dream of having. For a guy in his fifties, he really had it all going for him—thick waves of dark brown hair speckled with a few gleaming strands of silver, a chiseled face with a rich, tanned skin that spoke of his Italian heritage. He was a good-looking man and would probably stay that way for a very long time. I glanced behind his desk at the family photo on the wall. His wife—totally stunning—used to be a model. I'd read that was how they met. They looked so happy together, their arms lovingly placed around their only daughter, Kelly—another beauty.

Apparently, she worked with Justin, but we hadn't met many of each other's colleagues yet. Justin had spoken to Jules once, but that was about it. We were both too busy to attend each other's work functions, and since starting at Echelon, I hadn't had the time to pop into Torrence Records to visit either my husband or my father.

"Good afternoon, Mr. DeMarco."

"Please, how many times must I tell you to call me Enrique." He indicated the chair in front of his desk. My heels tapped on the wood as I walked toward it. Enrique's keen eyes traveled down my body, no doubt assessing my outfit. I perched on the edge of the shiny leather chair and looked up at him. He gave me an approving smile, but it didn't do much to quell my nerves. Enrique traveled a lot, so people were hyper aware of his presence when he was actually in LA. From what I could gather, the staff really loved him, but even after a year, I still felt like a newbie and he put me on edge. I so badly wanted to impress him, prove that he'd made the right decision in hiring me.

Threading his fingers together, he placed them lightly on his desk and shone me a warm smile.

"How are you doing, Sarah?"

I liked his accent. Even though he'd been raised in the States, he'd managed to retain his Italian lilt. It was kind of sexy.

I couldn't help a blush as I answered him. "Good. I love it here. Thank you so much for the opportunity."

"Julian is very impressed with you."

"Oh, Jules is amazing. He's so talented, and I'm learning so much from him. He's a wonderful mentor."

The edge of Enrique's mouth tipped with a barely-there smile. "He thinks a few of your pieces are ready for the catwalk."

"Really?" I nearly fell off the chair. My body jolted when my voice pitched high. I perched my heels on the polished floor and laughed. "He…said that?"

"He met with me yesterday, showed me some of your pieces, and suggested you might like to accompany me to Las Vegas in a couple of weeks."

"For the show? The Vegas show?"

Enrique snickered, obviously finding my five-year-old enthusiasm amusing. I cleared my throat and willed my voice to calm the hell down.

"Sorry," I murmured. "This is just so exciting."

"Then it's settled. I will take you, Julian, and Franco from here, and Sasha, Colin, and Michael will join us from New York. You can help with setup and be backstage for the show. Here are the pieces I'd like you to bring." He handed me a sheet of paper. "And on Saturday night, you will accompany me to the after party."

"Wow," I whispered, taking the sheet and scanning the pictures. He liked my cobalt dress! Holy crap, he liked the dress!

"And for all your hard work, I will even let you have Sunday to enjoy Vegas."

I giggled. I couldn't help it.

"Feel free to bring a friend with you, if you'd like."

"Really?"

"It's your first show. You must have someone there to celebrate with you."

My smile was so huge it took over my entire face.

He chuckled and picked up the gold pen on his desk, tapping it lightly on his palm. "Do you have someone in mind?"

"Yes." I nodded, my voice firm and sure.

I was taking my husband. This show was an opportunity to get Justin away from his work. I had Sunday off, a whole day to enjoy Vegas. A whole new chance to revive what Justin and I used to have together. All we needed was to get out of LA for a few days. Once the show was done, I could give him my full attention. Who knew what we could get up to after the party.

I pressed my lips together, quelling the smile threatening to expose me. Three nights and a full day off in Vegas...I was sure we could entertain ourselves quite nicely.

EIGHT

JUSTIN

"Y-yes, Mom, work is g-great." I tried to keep my voice light as I assured my mother that I was doing the best job I could. Our weekly call consisted of the same questions and answers every time. It was like this weird routine.

How is work? Good.

How is school? Great.

Are you managing to juggle it all? Of course I am.

My standard answers and the truth were not always in line, but it's what my mother needed to hear. She couldn't handle bad news like she used to. No one in the Doyle house could. The star member in our family was buried under six feet of dirt. It was kind of hard for his golden coat to shine from down there.

A sick guilt that tasted old and stale simmered in my gut. Blake shouldn't be where he was. He should be the one on the phone chatting to our mother and reassuring her that life was beautiful.

Movement outside my door caught my eye. I spotted her red hair before I saw her face, and bolted upright.

"Mom, I gotta go. Jane's here."

"Give her our love." Mom's voice wavered.

"I will," I croaked, smoothing down my tie before ending the call.

"Hey." Jane stepped into my office. Her emerald eyes didn't shine as bright these days. I studied the contours of her white face, noticing the permanent strain around her eyes and the sad dip of her rosebud lips. She'd always been beautiful, but it wasn't the same. A piece of her had been stolen on her wedding day, and no matter how hard I wished for it, I couldn't give it back to her.

I cleared my throat and stood from my desk, walking around to give her a slightly awkward hug. It was the kind where you pat the back and pull free as quickly as possible.

"S-s-so, I have the stuff here f-for you." I turned to my shelves and pulled off the stack of Chaos posters Marcus had given me.

"Thank you so much. The kids will love this. I just couldn't think what to give them as an end-of-year present."

"Rock s-star s-signatures are always a g-good way to go."

Her lips twitched with a micro-smile.

Man, her face used to light like the sun when Blake was around. I couldn't remember the last time I heard her laugh. My brother would be so disappointed in me. I didn't need to hear it from him to know that he'd want me to look after his girl. I was doing a terrible job. She looked thin and lost...depleted. I knew exactly how she felt, but I couldn't voice any of it. The thick, black emotions were clogged in my throat, coating my interior like a viscous poison.

"So, um..." I ran a hand over my curls. "Y-you looking f-forward to s-summer break?"

"Not really." She shrugged, holding the posters like a big, uncomfortable teddy bear. "I'm not sure what I'm going to do with myself. I've only got three weeks left before my students leave and then I'm..." She shrugged again. "I don't know."

The anniversary of Blake's death was approaching. She'd be in the middle of summer break when it happened. I closed my eyes, not wanting to think about it. How could it have only been a year? It felt like a freaking decade.

The horrific incident had sliced years off all our lives.

Jane licked her lower lip, looking awkward as she tipped back on her heels. Her thin legs were hidden beneath a long, floaty skirt. The belt around her hips was looped tighter than usual. I could tell by the markings that she was having to make it smaller just to keep it from sliding down her legs.

Geez, I was the world's worst brother.

It should have been me in that ditch.

I swallowed, tortured by images of Sarah standing next to Blake with that hollow look in her eyes. He would have done better though. He would have held her close, talked her through it. I couldn't say anything, so I just stood in my office like an idiot, internally bleeding as I watched the love of Blake's life try to hold herself together.

"I-I'll walk you out, shall I?"

"Sure." Jane nodded, obviously relieved by the suggestion.

We stepped into the corridor and shuffled toward the elevators. "How's Sarah doing?"

"G-good. Busy with work, of course. Y-you should stop by s-sometime."

"I will. Once I get through these last chaotic weeks. End-of-year stuff is always crazy."

"I-I don't know how you do it."

"Eleven- and twelve-year-olds aren't so bad...and kids seem to love music, so..." She sighed.

I could tell by the look on Jane's face that she was remembering my brother. He was the one who had encouraged her to pursue music in the first place. She was gearing up to study English and history, but halfway through her degree, she'd switched to music and teaching middle school instead of high school. She'd been overjoyed by the move. I wondered if she still felt the same way.

We slowed to a stop outside the elevators.

"Well, g-good luck."

"You too. Are you taking a summer break?"

"Not sure. Sarah and I h-haven't really t-talked about it yet. I-I'll let you know though."

"Don't worry about it. I wouldn't want to be a third wheel."

I grabbed her shoulder before she could turn away and step into the elevator. "You never would be. J-Jane, you'll always be f-family."

Her sad eyes glistened with a smile as she mouthed, "Thank you."

I let her go, and she disappeared behind the thick metal doors. Kneading the back of my neck, I listened to the elevator descend before spinning back to my office.

Kelly, the lady who started at Torrence a few months after me, smiled when I passed reception, her keen eyes reading everything. I forced a tight grin and picked up my pace. I didn't want her to see my shame, and the incredibly lousy job I was doing at filling the gap Blake had left behind.

NINE

SARAH

The grocery bags tried to cut off the circulation in my arms. I lugged them into the house and dropped the canvas sacks onto the counter then blew a strand of hair off my face. I hadn't been shopping in weeks. Work was all-consuming. Both Justin and I were constantly busy, and it was a fight to get fresh food in the house. Takeout was more common than anything, but that night, I was determined to cook something decent. I had my Vegas news to share, and I wanted Justin to actually sit and hear me.

So, no laptops, no cellphones—nothing was

going to interrupt us. We *needed* a decent night together.

Walking across the chaotic living room, I stepped over a pile of law books, nearly impaled myself with a sewing needle, and managed to just avoid knocking over a half-drunken cup of coffee. I lifted up the cold mug and wondered how many days it'd been sitting there. The house looked like a garbage dump. I hated it, but I just hadn't found the time (or motivation) to actually do anything about it. I'd never really wanted to move into this place. It was so square and sterile with no quirks or special characteristics—just a new, shiny house with no soul.

But when my parents had offered it to us, I didn't want to be the one to argue. It was a great opportunity, and we couldn't pass it up just to satisfy my creative eccentricities. So, I'd hugged my father with an excited giggle and shown him how much the gesture meant to me.

I pulled Justin's hoodie off the end of the couch and draped it over my arm. Stopping at the stereo, I pressed play and smiled when Mika's voice filtered into the air. Jane had introduced me to the artist in my freshman year at college. Actually, that's how we met. She was listening to his music and I really liked it, so I asked who was playing. We got chatting and before long, we were sorority sisters, and the friendship blossomed into the BFF kind.

I swayed my hips to the beat of "Good Guys" while I threw Justin's hoodie up the stairs and proceeded into the kitchen to start unpacking groceries. Nudging empty takeout boxes closer to the trash can, I hummed along to the music while I tidied and put away. The song always made me nostalgic...sad. I didn't know why I liked it so much. I should have hated it because it made me think of Blake. But that's why I loved it. He was a good guy, right down to his core.

I missed him.

I missed his influence and the impact he had on Justin's life.

Nothing had been the same since Jane's nightmare wedding day.

As usual, tears tried to blind me. I sniffed them back and thought about work—the one area in my life that was going beautifully.

Heading to work each day and hanging out with Jules was the closest thing to fun I could find. I thrived on it, pouring all my emotion into sketches, patterns, fabrics, tucks, folds, pins, needles, threads—anything to do with creating beautiful clothes for beautiful bodies.

And all my hard work had paid off. An excited smile stretched my mouth wide. I couldn't wait to tell Justin. I wondered what he'd say.

Probably not much.

My smile faltered and I swallowed.

Reaching for the chopping board, I placed it next to the sink then washed my hands and got ready to make Justin's favorite Indian curry. The lady who used to look after him when he was little gave me the recipe as a wedding gift.

"You'll keep your boy happy with this one. Chicken tikka masala is his favorite." Her thick Indian accent had made me smile. I'd lovingly tucked the recipe away...and hadn't pulled it out once since we returned from England.

My insides twittered and jumped as I chopped and sautéed. The kitchen soon smelled rich with spices, Mika's voice accompanying the swirl of creativity in the air. By the time Justin walked through the door, I was dancing away to "Emily."

I hadn't even heard him walk in. My hips were jiggling as I stirred the bright orange mixture. Stopping to check the rice, I tapped the wooden spoon on the side of the pot then spun around, using it as a microphone to sing a little French with Mika.

Justin was leaning against the counter watching me with his arms crossed over his chest. His smile showed off a little of the guy I met in college. I could have basked in that affectionate glow all day.

I jerked when I saw him then giggled. "Hey."

"Hi, Sparks." His voice always had such a calming effect on me. It was quiet and smooth, carrying on the air with a gentle lilt that reminded me of dandelion florets floating on the breeze.

We grinned at each other, and I swear I saw a glint of hot desire flash through his gaze. His eyes whisked down my body, but then he jerked tall and turned away from me.

He hadn't touched me since that last time. That's right, I remembered the last time we'd had sex. How could I forget? It'd been the early hours of the morning. The sleepy, half-awake kind of sex where you feel like you're floating on some euphoric cloud, caught between fantasy and reality. I'd woken in the night, desire pulsing through me after a dream that would have made Hugh Hefner blush. I didn't know what had brought it on, but I needed release. I kissed Justin awake and we had hot, passionate sex. He pounded into me—hard, fast, and deeper than he ever had before, a shocking mix of pleasure with a touch of pain. The orgasm that rocked me was like nothing I'd had before. My sharp cries surprised us both.

Justin pulled out of me, spilling his seed on the sheets and shuddering like he'd just been punched in the belly.

I sat up to talk to him, but he lurched off the bed, puffing and running his hands through his hair.

"Justin?" I'd whispered as he fled to the door. He turned and gave me a wrecked kind of half-smile that radiated torment rather than joy. And then he went downstairs. As soon as I heard the toilet flush, I crept down to check on him. He was sitting at his desk with the lamp on, his nose buried in a thick textbook.

I'd cried myself to sleep that night, and hadn't had it in me to try again.

But that was going to change.

I turned back to the curry and kept stirring. If I waited for him to initiate sex, I'd be waiting a long time. I didn't know how to reach him...and it scared me.

Justin sauntered back into the kitchen to pour himself a glass of water. I studied his profile as he gulped it down, turning away when he swiveled to look at me.

"How was work?" I kept my eyes on the bubbling curry, breathing in the rich scent like it would somehow give me courage.

"Good."

"Anything interesting from your day?"

He placed the glass down and sighed before spinning to face me. "Just the usual—contracts, law stuff, studying, and then more law stuff." He snickered, running a hand through his curls. His enthusiasm over taking the job in the first place had certainly waned.

Who was I kidding? Everything had waned since Blake's death.

"Jane stopped by to grab some Chaos posters for her kids."

"Oh, yeah?" Guilt singed me. I hadn't called in over a week. "How's she doing?"

Justin shrugged. "You know."

The topic sucked all conversation from the room. I licked my lips and kept stirring.

Sometimes I wanted to grab Justin's shoulders and shake him...hard. I wanted to yell in his face that there was life after Blake. That he couldn't wear Jane's heartache like a trench coat.

But I wouldn't do that.

Yelling at Justin would only drive him away. I was barely holding on as it was; I didn't want to do anything that might fracture our threadbare relationship.

I put on a smile and went for upbeat. "I'm making your favorite tonight."

"I thought something smelled good." His eyebrows rose, and I caught a glimpse of his old smile again.

My insides trilled, and I shifted aside so he could take a look in the pot.

"Chicken tikka masala." He sniffed the air. "What's the occasion?"

I shrugged, giving him a playful smile. "I have good news."

"Really?" His eyebrows dipped.

"Uh-huh." I forced a bright smile before he could step away from me. Justin didn't like news anymore. He didn't trust it. Even though I'd said the word *good*, he still shied away from anything that might disrupt the protective little world he'd created around himself. "My designs got selected for the Echelon Show in Vegas!" I squealed.

"No way." Justin laughed and wrapped his arms around me. My feet left the floor, and I buried my face in the crook of his neck. Damn, it felt good. "I'm so proud of you." He swung me around once before placing me down and grinning at me. "You deserve it."

"Thank you."

He brushed his thumb over my lips before gently pinching my chin. "Is it your…wedding stuff?"

"No." The timer beeped, and I was forced to step away from him and check the rice. Turning off the gas, I moved the pot to the counter before lifting the lid and giving it a stir. "It's the fall line, so…"

"Okay." He nodded and gave me a closed-mouth smile.

The last wedding dress I'd designed was for some well-to-do friend of Enrique DeMarco's. It had actually been an old design that Jules had found in my folder. He'd loved it and shown it to Enrique without my say-so.

My ultimate dream was to start up my own wedding business. I'd provide the client with everything, like a wedding designer/planner person.

The original idea had been to work at Echelon Fashion for five years, saving my guts out, and then I'd start up my own company.

The only problem was I hadn't been able to draw another dress since Blake died. I just couldn't bring myself to go there. Weddings didn't make me think of joy and magic anymore. All they did was remind me of a motorcycle accident and one of the best guys I knew bleeding out on an English country road.

"Can you grab two plates?" I pointed at the cupboard.

Justin did as I asked and placed them on the counter beside me. I dished up the meal, adding a splash of bright green beans to the side of each plate. Carrying the dishes out, I set them down while Justin grabbed the cutlery and two wineglasses.

I waited for him to pop the cork and pour before lifting my glass. "To Vegas."

He grinned and tapped his glass against mine. "To you."

A blush warmed my skin, and I took a sip. "Do you want to know the best part?"

"Sure." Justin flicked the napkin over his knee.

"I've been given an extra ticket. You, my darling husband, are going to be there with me to celebrate. We'll be staying at The Venetian in a gorgeous room overlooking the Strip. You can come to the show on Saturday afternoon, and then there's drinks and stuff afterwards. But all day Sunday is ours." I gripped his wrist and gave him my excited face. "Vegas, Justin! We've never been there. It's gonna be such a blast!"

"Are you…" He let out a breathy laugh. "Are you sure you don't want to take your mom or Maria instead? You know how much they love fashion."

I sat back, desperately trying to hide my disappointment behind a bright smile. "I could, but I really wanted you to be there. You've always been my biggest cheerleader and it just… It seems right."

His smile was soft with gratitude before he looked down at his plate and licked his bottom lip. "So, when is it?"

"About two weeks. I have to leave on Thursday after work to help with setup and all that kind of stuff, but then you can fly in on Friday night or Saturday morning, and we've got the weekend."

His head bobbed while I talked, but he wouldn't

look up at me. Nudging a piece of chicken with his fork, he started mumbling, "Two weeks, deadline thirteenth, exam week after?" He reached for his phone to check something. "Yeah, yeah, I can probably do that."

"Cool." I grinned, trying not to let his calm, unenthusiastic manner bother me. Spinning the fork between my thumb and index finger, nerves ate at me as I looked down at my plate. "You know this will be our first holiday since… In a really long time. I think it'll be good for us to get away from work."

He tipped his head and looked at me. "Well, *you'll* still be working."

I blushed and forced another grin. "Yeah, but on Sunday, I'm all yours. And maybe being out of LA will be really good, you know. We can just…focus on each other."

My voice was so hopeful, silently begging him to let me back in. Were my eyes doing the same thing? I tentatively reached for his arm, rubbing my fingers over the fine, dark hairs.

His lips were tight as he reached for my hand and gave it a little squeeze. "You're right," he croaked. "It'll be great."

TEN

JUSTIN

My phone hadn't stopped ringing all week. I picked it up and barked into the receiver, "What?"

My brusque tone had Kelly whistling at me. "Did I catch you at a bad time?"

Closing my eyes, I drooped my head and sighed. "S-sorry. Busy day."

She chuckled. "Don't sweat it. I was just calling to let you know that Mr. Torrence would like to see you."

"What? Why?" I couldn't help the whiny way I said it. My brain was fried having worked around the clock all week so I could turn my phone off in

Vegas. The way Sarah looked at me when she said we needed to focus on each other nearly broke my heart. I'd spent most of my life not living up to people's expectations, but Sarah had always been different. Probably because she'd never expected much from me...until I became her husband.

I wanted to be there for her, be the man she deserved. After eleven months of slogging it out, I still wasn't sure I was capable.

"Do you want me to defer him?"

I rolled my eyes. "Like that would ever f-fly." Scanning my schedule, I looked over my workload and cringed. "W-when does he want t-to see me?"

"He's free between five and six this afternoon."

"I'm supposed to be leaving for V-Vegas at six thirty."

"So, defer him."

"I-I can't." I sighed. "I-I'll just m-make new arrangements."

"Are you sure?"

I closed my eyes and nodded. "I-it's not worth pissing off the b-big man."

"What about pissing off the wife?"

"Kelly," I chided.

"You're right. None of my business. Enjoy your meeting." She hung up, and I scowled at my phone.

Damn it, that woman was sharp. I hadn't told anyone about sneaking off to Vegas. I made one little slip-up and Kelly put everything together in thirty seconds flat. Her father was Sarah's boss—the owner of Echelon Fashion—and he would no doubt be in Vegas for the weekend as well.

I'd never met the man, but I'd seen pictures. The guy was highly regarded in fashion circles. Sarah had nearly lost her mind when she first got the call inviting her in for an interview. She hadn't even applied for a job, but her design teacher at Stanford had sent her work to a friend at Echelon. They showed it to Enrique DeMarco, and he offered Sarah a job. She deserved it. She deserved every good thing life could throw at her. I was so incredibly proud of my girl.

The weight inside me, the one I couldn't seem to shift, felt heavier than usual. Sarah had kissed me good-bye yesterday morning, and I'd returned to an empty house. It had almost been a relief, which made me feel like the world's worst husband. But four walls and no humans meant zero expectations. I didn't have to put on a smile or fight the urge to take Sarah in my arms and make love to her.

She was so beautiful...and I was so undeserving.

I wished I could explain it to her. There was so much going on inside me, and I couldn't get any of it out. I was worried that if I even whispered a word of what I felt, the dam would bust right open, and I'd never recover.

Snatching up my pen, I pulled the contract I'd been revising back toward me and found my place. The words drew me away from fallout. I focused on the boring text, losing myself in a sea of legal jargon in the hope of keeping my head above water for just a little longer.

*****

I knocked on Everett Torrence's door then tugged down my jacket and made sure I looked presentable.

"Come in, son," he called from inside.

Like my father, Everett had the ability to paralyze me. I pushed the heavy mahogany door open and shuffled inside, taking a seat in the plump chair opposite him. Resting the iPad on my legs, I tried to smile at my father-in-law.

He frowned at my attempt, shaking his head and gazing out the window. "How are things going for you?"

"Uh…" I cleared my throat. "F-fine, sir."

Where was he going with this?

Threading his fingers together, he knocked them on the desk in front of him. "You enjoying your job?"

"Of course," I lied.

How could I possibly tell him the truth?

Actually, no, I hate it with a passion. Couldn't think of anything more boring than law, but see, when you offered me this job I knew it would make everybody happy. And then I need the income, see, so I can save up and help Sarah get started with her wedding business. The one she doesn't seem that keen on anymore.

Everett smiled at me, obviously liking my answer. "Good." He slapped the table. "That's excellent news. The company is expanding every year, and I don't like investing money in people who don't want to be here. So..." He slapped the table again. "I'd like to increase your work hours."

"I-increase?"

"Yeah, well, I'm leaving for Bora Bora next Friday. I'll be gone for a week, and I have a few important things I want wrapped up before I go. Being away always puts a little more pressure on my exec team. To ease their load, I'm passing on jobs to various underlings in the company." He chuckled and winked after he said the word *underlings*.

I forced a smile.

"Clay wants to give you more responsibility and I've agreed. Now we've just picked up a new band—The Euphonics. I'll email you all the information, and I want you to run the whole process this time. You draw up their contracts, negotiate the terms. Marcus will help you. Don't get them to sign anything until after Clay's given them the once-over."

"But..."

"I know you have a lot on your plate with the studying as well, but I'm sure you can handle it. Now, Clay needs first drafts by Monday, before you and Marcus go in to meet with them, and I want everything finalized before I fly out. That way, we can get started with scheduling while I'm away."

"I c-can't this w-weekend."

Everett's face flashed with a frown. "We'll get Marcus to do the talking in the meetings. You don't have to worry about that." His kind smile did nothing to dull the insult.

I ignored its bruising effect and tried again. "That's g-gonna t-take me s-s-some time to p-put together."

"I know. That's why I'm giving you the weekend."

"B-but…"

"Is there a problem, son?" he snapped, impatience radiating from his scowl.

I should have said yes. I should have stuttered my way through a passionate argument about needing to be with my wife. But I sucked at those. So instead, I *thanked him* for the opportunity then shuffled my ass out of that office, work piled so high around me I couldn't see through it.

Stepping into the elevator with a heavy sigh, I checked my watch. "Shit."

I wouldn't make my flight. As soon as I reached my office, I called Sarah.

"Hey." Her voice was bright. "Are you at the airport?"

"I got caught up in meetings. I'm not going to make it."

There was a chilling pause before she quietly squeaked, "Okay."

Guilt doused me, setting off a quick fire in my belly that threatened to turn my legs to ash.

I flopped into my chair. "So, um…" I scratched my eyebrow. "I'll try to make it tomorrow?"

Did I mean that? Or was I quietly hoping she'd give me an easy out?

She didn't.

Instead, she used that low, sweet tone that worked like a sucker punch. "You said you'd come, Justin."

"I will. I…just have a lot on my plate right now." Her silent response sent my singed gut into a spiral. "Sparks, come on."

"I have to go. It's crazy here. Last-minute stuff. You know how it is. Good luck with your workload."

"I'll see you tomorrow," I promised, hoping to suck that disappointment from her tone.

"Yeah. See ya."

She didn't believe me.

Hell, I barely did.

After hanging up, I punched in the airline number with a sharp sigh then rebooked my flight to Vegas. If I pulled an all-nighter, I could hopefully fit in the work and still keep my wife happy.

Who was I kidding?

I hadn't made my wife happy since Blake died.

I never expected the hole he left behind to be quite so big. There was no warning for that kind of thing. You don't expect to lose your best friend at the age of twenty-two. No one could have prepared me for the aching sadness and guilt so mind-numbing it threatened to swallow me whole.

In that moment, I felt like I couldn't be anything to anybody.

And it made me want to shut down completely.

ELEVEN

SARAH

The show was a huge success. People loved Echelon's new line, and my stuff received the kind of praise I'd always dreamed of. I got to stand on stage with Enrique and the other designers. We bowed together and waved at the cameras. The models gathered around us, glowing at the success of it all. What a dream—glitz, glamor, success, praise... and I couldn't even manage a genuine smile.

The seat I'd reserved for Justin sat vacant the entire show. I peeked out every time I sent a new model down the catwalk. And every time, his empty seat stuck out as if there were a spotlight on it. His broken promises felt like bullet wounds. There was a time he would have dropped everything to be with me. I used to be his number one priority…and now I was his last.

Work. That was all he freaking cared about.

A mellow jazz band played in the corner of the party room. It was a massive ballroom on the ground floor of The Venetian. It was filled with smiles, expensive clothes, and champagne glasses. Waiters circulated the room, serving drinks and nibbles—fancy food art that you could eat in one bite.

I shook my head at an approaching waiter. I wasn't hungry. Jules stood beside me, flirting with some guy he'd just met. I shuffled away from them and found myself next to Michael. He smiled down at me, holding up his champagne glass so I could clink mine against his.

"Good job tonight. You were amazing."

"So were you." I tipped my head.

His eyes warmed before skimming down my body. I was in a dark turquoise dress Jules made. The bodice consisted of two thick strips that covered each breast and were secured with a beaded piece of fabric that circled my neck. The skirt rippled around my body, ending mid-thigh and giving the dress a cute, party feel. I'd paired it with some elegant, open-toe heels that gave my short frame another five inches. It was probably one of my sexier outfits, but Enrique had stressed how good he'd wanted us to look, and Jules had been very convincing.

I probably shouldn't have enjoyed Michael's gaze so much. It just felt like such a compliment after my husband had rejected me. Michael was a married man, so his brief admiration didn't make me feel uncomfortable. His wife was back in New York, looking after their babies. I just wanted to take it for what it was. I looked hot, and he noticed.

The band started playing "Girl Put Your Records On," so I turned to watch the singer step up to the mic. Her long fingers curved around the stand while her shapely body swayed to the beat. Her fitted leopard-skin dress and six-inch heels elongated her legs, made her breasts pop, and turned the woman into a sexy diva. If she'd put that outfit together herself, she sure knew how to look good. And that voice, so rich and powerful—like Ella Fitzgerald or Aretha Franklin. I could have listened to it all night.

"Wonderful job tonight, young lady." A woman I didn't know approached me with a dazzling smile. I shook her hand and thanked her.

Enrique hovered behind her sparkly dress, giving me signals that told me to impress the woman. So, I did my best, putting on the show I was so good at. She laughed at my compliments on her gown then told me I was the sweetest thing. Michael pitched in with a few comments that made her blush.

After ten minutes of painful schmoozing, she glided away on Enrique's arm to flirt with someone else. I'd forgotten her name by the time she reached them. Michael's eyes bulged at me, and I gave him a halfhearted smile and sipped my champagne. Exhaustion tugged at me. I hadn't slept well the night before; nerves about the show and disappointment over my husband's no-show made it impossible to relax.

I didn't really feel like partying either. If I was honest, all I wanted was Justin's arms around me, to be transported back to that little hotel in Brighton where we spent the day making love. Back to a time where the world was perfect and my husband still wanted me.

Tears threatened to sear my eyeballs and make my mascara run, so I stepped toward the door.

"You okay?" Michael called after me.

"Fine." I shone him what I hoped was a believable smile before slipping from the room.

My heels sank into the plush carpet as I strode through the casino. The gaming floor felt like a quiet oasis compared to the packed fanfare of the Echelon event. I was sick of the plastic-coated conversation and trying to put on a brave face when all I felt like doing was drowning in a tub full of tears. I wandered beneath the opulent chandeliers, around the blackjack tables, and past the roulette wheels until I spotted a dimly lit bar.

"Don't Know Why" by Norah Jones oozed from the hidden speakers, and I let the words coat me. A mixture of anger and sadness swirled inside my stomach. Why hadn't Justin come? Why did he keep hiding from me?

I slid onto one of the padded stools and smiled

at the waiter.

He rested his arms on the bar and grinned. "What can I get you, sweetie?"

"Just a house white, thanks."

"Gotcha." He winked and moved to fill my order. He reminded me a little of Blake, that easy charisma and charm. He had a similar physique to Justin and really suited the fitted dress pants and white shirt rolled up to his elbows. It showed off the muscles of his forearms.

I remembered lying in bed with Justin, tracing those muscles. I used to love the way they moved when he touched me, the shift and pull while his fingers worked their magic inside me. I'd trail my hands up and down his arm before clutching him and crying out.

Opening my purse, I checked my phone and noticed a message from Justin. My nose tingled as I dialed my voicemail.

"I'm so, so sorry, Sparks. I pulled an all-nighter and fell asleep. I missed my flight again. Call me as soon as you get this, okay? I'm sorry." He sounded cut-up enough.

Gritting my teeth, I forced my simmering anger away then lifted the phone back to my ear when it started ringing.

"Hey." Justin sounded tired, his voice husky and deep.

"Hi." I didn't know what to say to him. Gone were the days of conversation where two hours could slip by without us noticing.

"How was the show?"

"Good," I clipped. "Huge success."

"I knew it would be." I could hear the smile in his voice but struggled to match it.

Instead, I gave him a heavy sigh.

"I'm sorry, Sarah," he whispered. "I'm so snowed under right now. But I should have been there."

"Doesn't matter." I shrugged. "I get it. Work's insane for me too."

"I let you down."

The words *yeah, you did* sat on my tongue, but I closed my lips over them. He'd spent his life feeling that way, and I wasn't going to jump on his parents' bandwagon with stupidly high expectations that could never be reached. Since Blake died, Justin seemed even more obsessed with becoming the perfect child. It was painful to watch.

I flicked my hair over my shoulder and rested my elbows on the bar. "Did you get through all your work?"

"I got lumped with a whole new project on Friday afternoon. I've been going all day."

"Are you sure you can't still come?" My voice pitched on the last word, hope making it higher than usual. "My room is gorgeous, and we could spend tomorrow together. Remember how we used to spend all day in bed… That seaside hotel in England?"

His silence told me everything I needed to know, but I put in one last-ditch effort anyway. I didn't realize how desperate I'd been feeling.

"Come on, if you leave for the airport right now,

you could be here by midnight. I'll wait up for you. You can work on the plane."

"This is a really important opportunity your dad's given me, Sarah. I can't just drop the ball. This has to be perfect."

I clenched my jaw, my nose twitching as I willed myself not to cry.

"I, um…you know, if I work really hard tonight and tomorrow before you get back, I'll be all yours when you return. Let's have dinner together tomorrow night. I could take you out. Once all my work's done, I'll be more relaxed."

No, you won't.

Tears burned my eyes. I looked to the ceiling in an attempt to fight them. Pressing my trembling lips together, I bobbed my head and replied, "Yeah, sounds nice."

He knew it wasn't enough. We both did.

But neither of us could say it.

"I love you, Sarah."

"Love you too." I hung up before he heard the tears in my voice.

How could words that mean so much sound so hollow?

We'd been saying them to each other for years, meaning it with every fiber of our being. And now I wasn't sure if love could even hold us together.

Our wedding anniversary was just around the corner, and I didn't even know if we were going to celebrate it. What was there to celebrate?

So far, our marriage had consisted of two perfect weeks, followed by tragedy, silence, emptiness, loneliness, living around each other like we were scared to get too close and actually feel something.

Justin and I had been using work as the excuse for everything. We'd been hiding away in our own little worlds. This Vegas weekend would have been my chance to open up and be honest with him. I'd been prepping myself to lay it all bare, tell him how much I needed him. How much I missed him.

He knew it. He saw the look on my face when I first invited him.

Yet he backed away. He fell asleep.

Once again, he used work as an excuse not to fix us.

Tears slid down my cheeks without me noticing. The bartender set down my glass with a kind smile. I looked at the pale yellow liquid and shook my head.

"Actually, can I have a shot of vodka instead?"

His mouth tugged up at the side. "Sure thing, gorgeous."

Drumming my fingers on the bar, I waited for my drink, yearning for a taste of oblivion. If I couldn't have sex with my husband, I might as well get rip-roaring drunk.

TWELVE

JUSTIN

Spend the day in bed together.

That's what she'd wanted to do.

She never outright said it, but I knew her well enough to know what she meant. I wouldn't be flying to Vegas to check out the sights. I'd be flying to Vegas to try and make up for the last few months of dry-docking. She wanted us tangled in the sheets, body painting each other with invisible ink.

I wished I could tell her what her touch did to me. I wished I could voice the truth that every time I slipped inside her, I was hit with a scarring image of my brother's mangled body in that damn ditch. I should have been there for him. It had been his wedding day. He'd been edgy and distracted…in no condition to ride a motorbike, especially the way he rode one.

I didn't know if I could ever get over the fact that while I was orgasming, Blake was bleeding out.

I didn't deserve sex anymore. Especially after the last time.

I didn't deserve Sarah's affection.

It should have been me on that road. Blake had always been the better man, yet he was the one taken.

How could I tell Sarah any of that? How I could excuse the way I behaved the last time I couldn't resist her?

Her cry of pain would live in my mind forever—taunting me, reminding me that I should have been the dead man. I'd thrust too deep, taken her too hard in an attempt to drive thoughts of a sunken skull and lifeless eyes from my mind. I'd used her body like some kind of sick therapy and ended up hurting her.

I'd wanted to apologize, beg for her forgiveness, but I hadn't been able to voice any of it. I couldn't admit how I really felt, or what was going on in my mind when I should have been enjoying her body.

I didn't want her sharing the guilt that swamped me every day. If I told her that sex took me right back to Blake's death, would she take onboard what I was feeling? If she hadn't considered it yet, I didn't want her thinking about the fact we were moaning in ecstasy while Blake was inhaling his last breath.

The best I could do was work hard and try to prove myself worthy of life. I was getting my law degree for my parents and working my ass off for my father-in-law.

But what was I doing for Sarah?

Fisting my curls with a sigh, I brought up her image on my phone. I'd taken it our senior year, the day she'd been offered the job at Echelon Fashion. She'd been radiant, and I'd captured her astounded joy perfectly.

I did remember that day at our seaside hotel in Brighton, England. Sarah's body was a wonderland, and I'd explored every inch of it. We'd been together for a while, so I already knew what made her high, but throughout our honeymoon, I took the time to drive her to a new plane. I don't know how many times we'd had sex that particular day, but we'd both fallen asleep completely sated...and were still up for more the next morning. I couldn't get enough of her back then.

I wanted more of her now, but the brain is a powerful weapon and Blake's death was tearing me away from the thing I craved most—my wife.

I needed to make it right.

Hell, I probably needed to tell her what was holding me back. Maybe talking would fix this. If I sold it right, I could protect her from any kind of guilt, and then we could get back to being the newlyweds we were supposed to be.

Dropping my phone, I pulled my chair closer to my desk and got back to work. Motivation fueled my energy. I was finishing those damn contracts before midnight then I was going to bed, getting a decent night's sleep and waking up refreshed so I could spend Sunday cleaning the house, cooking Sarah's favorite meal, and making sure that when she walked in our door, she knew exactly how much I loved her.

THIRTEEN

SARAH

The light in the room was dim, but the cracks of light peeking down the edge of the heavy drapes told me it was morning. My head crashed like a cymbal, the aching, foggy pain enough to make me seek oblivion again. I closed my eyes and softly groaned.

My mouth felt thick and crusty. My eyelids had been replaced with a dense kind of metal that was hard to manipulate. My insides acted like the Sahara Desert.

"Water," my mind croaked.

I rubbed my forehead with shaky fingers,

internally lecturing myself about the evils of alcohol. Drinking my sorrows away was never a good idea. To be honest, I'd never taken it that far before. Justin had always been there to stop me from being stupid.

Justin.

I rubbed my eyes. The pain I had been trying to escape the night before landed back on me tenfold. Rolling to my side, I tucked my hand under my chin, trying to escape the train wreck of thoughts screaming at me. How was I supposed to go home and face him? What would we say to each other?

"Would he even be home?" I inwardly grumbled, the bitterness tasting sharp and tangy in my mind.

I sighed. I didn't want to be like that. I couldn't lie there grumbling about my failing marriage and turning into a sniveling little whiner. I needed to get home, sit Justin down, and have an honest conversation with him.

We couldn't keep going the way we were. Something had to let up. We had to start committing some time to working on our relationship. I'd just have to say it to him straight.

Justin, this isn't working. We need to make some changes and get back on track. I love you, and I'm not willing to throw away our marriage.

An overwhelming urge to get home pulsed through me. Cracking my eyes open, I was about to turn and check the time when I made the most horrifying discovery of my life.

I gasped and jerked away from the person lying

next to me.

"Shit," I whispered.

My eyes were bugging out so wide it was almost hard to see. I gripped the covers to my body, suddenly aware I was naked.

"No." I shook my head, tears popping onto my lashes. "Oh, God, please no."

My entire body started trembling as vague images of hands, lips, and drunken moans wafted through the back of my mind. None of them were clear. It was like watching a movie out of focus. Fuzzy memories that weren't enough to give details, but were enough for me to know what I'd done. I wanted it to be a dream...a nightmare, whatever.

But life wasn't that kind.

"No." My voice shook as I scrambled off the bed. The sheet slipped down, exposing my naked torso. I gasped and tried to cover myself, but the man in the bed just let out a grunt then sighed.

He was still dead to the world, his handsome face relaxed and peaceful. Snatching my dress off the floor, I slipped it on, not bothering to secure the back properly. All I could think of was escape. With a cringe, I snatched my underwear and heels, clutching them to my chest before shuffling across the massive room. My purse was on the coffee table in the living area next to an empty bottle of champagne and two long-stemmed glasses. Sobs were shaking my stomach, making it hard to breathe.

I stumbled into the hallway and ran to the

elevator, pressing the button like I had a nervous tic.

"No, no, no," I kept whispering. Tears streaked my face. I jumped into the elevator and took it down to the twentieth floor. I don't know how I made it to my room; spots were blinding me when I shoved my keycard into the slot and lurched through the door.

I only just made it into the bathroom before hurling. I clutched the toilet bowl and threw up violently, my body heaving as I poured out my guilt and shame.

How could I have let that happen?

Justin was the only man I'd ever been with. How could I let someone else touch me that way? How could I betray the only man I loved?

"My husband," I whispered, spittle dripping from my bottom lip...or maybe it was tears.

My retching turned into whimpering sobs. Dropping to the cold tiles, I curled into a ball and slapped the floor until my palm stung.

"No," I sobbed. "No. Justin, I'm sorry."

I cried until it hurt to move. My stomach ached like I'd been doing sit-ups all night. My head pounded. But I stayed on those tiles. I didn't know how to get up and face it all. So I just lay there and let silent tears dribble off my face and onto the floor.

FOURTEEN

JUSTIN

The house looked amazing. For a place I'd never one hundred percent loved, it was looking pretty damn cool. I had set my alarm for six and gotten up right away. It'd taken me all morning, but I'd cleaned and tidied every inch of the place. If Sarah's parents came to visit in the next minute, I wouldn't have minded at all. I couldn't help feeling a touch of pride. Spending a few hours paying attention to our place had given me more satisfaction than an entire week at the office.

It felt good to take care of Sarah again. I'd always been a really attentive boyfriend, and I'd let the ball drop. Work and tragedy had taken over everything.

It was time for that to stop.

Taking off my sweaty shirt, I walked into the laundry and dumped it in the hamper before snatching a clean one out of the dryer. I paused in the doorway and spun back, emptying the entire dryer into a fresh basket and carrying it up to our bedroom. As I folded, images of Sarah flashed through my mind—the first time I saw her, the smile on her face that time we danced under the stars, the way she giggled that time I cooked her dinner. It'd been my first attempt—macaroni and cheese that tasted burned and looked more brown than yellow. She'd eaten it anyway, and I'd fallen just a little more in love.

My cooking had improved big time since then. She'd taught me so much.

I thought about the first time we'd made love. We'd skipped class one afternoon, and she'd taken me to her empty sorority house. She'd giggled nervously as I'd undressed her. I'd tried to act like I knew what I was doing, but we were both clueless virgins. We'd spent the afternoon figuring it out, and by the time I kissed her good-bye, I knew I wanted to marry her.

The sound of a key in the lock made me spin. She was home early.

Placing her pink T-shirt on the top of her pile, I turned from the bed and headed down the stairs, meeting her at the front door. She looked tired and pale. The shadows under her eyes and the way she winced when she dropped her bag on the floor had me concerned.

"Hey." I jumped off the last step and rushed over to her. "Are you okay?"

She gave me a tired smile and nodded. "Yeah, I'm fine."

Her eyes looked dead with sorrow. Kind of the way they did at Blake's funeral. I veered away from the memory, determined not to bring him into the moment. I'd been doing a lot of self-talk throughout the morning. If I wanted to make things work with Sarah, I had to take Blake out of the equation. It would be a struggle, I couldn't deny that, but maybe if I talked loud enough and long enough, I could make it work.

I skimmed her cheek with my thumb and gazed at her. "You're home early."

She shied away from my touch and looked to the floor. "I caught an earlier flight. Jules and the others were gambling and I just… I didn't feel like it." Dropping her keys on the table, she shrugged out of her denim jacket and hung it on the hook. Her hands were shaking.

I reached for her quivering fingers and gave them a tender squeeze. "Are you sure you're okay?"

"I'm just not feeling very well," she whispered. Her eyes glassed over and she blinked rapidly before stepping past me. Jerking to a stop, she scanned the open-plan living area, from the spotless kitchen counter to the clutter-free floor and plumped pillows on the sofa.

"Wow." She said it like a sigh. "This place looks amazing."

"I know it doesn't make up for me bailing on you, but I really wanted to do something to apologize. Work keeps getting the better of me. I know I can't keep doing this to us, and I—"

"It's okay." She shook her head, staring at our enlarged wedding photo on the wall. It'd been a gift from her mother and was hanging there when we got back from our honeymoon. Neither of us had the heart to take it down, but I didn't think either of us loved it. We probably would have, if the memory hadn't been bathed in tragedy. Funny how Blake's death could extend so far, killing one of the most memorable days of our lives in the process.

Sarah caught me gazing at her and forced a tight smile. "I get that work's busy. It's the same for me, too."

"I know, but I still wanted to make it up to you. I'm going to cook you dinner and maybe we can..." My voice trailed off, trepidation working like a hand around my throat. I swallowed and made myself smile. "This is our night, Sparks." Heading for the stereo, I selected the playlist I'd created earlier.

"Where I Belong" was the first song I chose. A Lindsey Ray concert had been our first date. She'd performed an acoustic set in an open field—her, a guitar, and lovesick couples dancing on the grass. Sarah and I had shuffled beneath the stars and fallen in love.

Tears lined Sarah's lashes as she stared at the stereo then dragged her gaze to my face.

"What is it?" My concern spiked again, and I rushed to her side.

"I love this song," she whispered.

My worries eased, and I gave her a relaxed smile. Taking her wrist, I led her to an open space in the living room then drew her against me. She fitted into my arms so perfectly. Her small fingers threaded behind my neck, and she pressed her head against my chest.

I started swaying, leading her in a slow dance.

And she started crying.

Her tears were soft at first, soaking into my T-shirt like slow raindrops sliding down a pane of glass. I didn't understand them. I hoped they were happy tears.

Her husband was finally giving her the attention she deserved. Maybe she'd been bottling everything up like I had, and she couldn't contain it anymore. My long-awaited kindness was working like a corkscrew, freeing her pent-up emotions so they overflowed like bubbling champagne.

My guilt was thick and metallic. I tried not to let it swallow me whole, but I couldn't deny the truth. I'd waited too long to get my act together. I'd failed her, and now she was whimpering against me. It hurt my heart to listen to her.

Blinking, I pressed my lips to Sarah's head and kept swaying. "I love you, Sparks."

My whispered words made her shudder. A fresh wave of tears took her, but these weren't the soft, gentle kind. They were ugly sobs. She wriggled free of my arms and covered her mouth, turning away from me and stumbling into the dining room.

"Sarah?" I lurched after her.

Her hands slapped onto the back of the wooden chair, and she gripped it until her knuckles turned white.

I didn't know what the hell was going on, but I hated seeing my wife distressed. Gently running my hand up her back, I squeezed the nape of her neck and whispered, "Baby, what is it?"

"I cheated on you." She choked out the words.

My brain froze for a second. I must have heard her wrong.

I snickered—a disbelieving, breathy sound. "What?"

She spun to face me, her blotchy cheeks warning me that I wasn't going to like the truth. Pulling in a ragged breath, she tried again. "I slept with someone last night. I'm sorry. I…"

I let her go. I stepped back from the world's most beautiful woman as if she were toxic. My heart started thrumming, sending a sick drumbeat coursing through my veins. I was suddenly filled with an army of marching soldiers ready to wipe me clean off the earth. Their boots pounded inside me, cutting off my ability to think straight.

I backed away from her until I crashed into the kitchen counter.

"Justin, I'm sorry," she whispered, sagging against the chair.

Rubbing my temple, I frowned at her, still trying to compute what the fuck was going on.

"Who?" I finally hissed then shot my hand into the air. "No, wait! I don't want to know." My voice turned low and hostile, my anger swerving out of control.

I gritted my teeth and tore my eyes away from her.

"Please, I'll tell you anything." Sarah stepped toward me. "I'll do whatever it takes to make this right."

"You slept with someone else!" I thundered.

She flinched at my roar. I'd never yelled at her before. Her face crested with agonized torment, but it wasn't enough to quell whatever the hell was going on inside me.

"I didn't mean to, Justin. I…"

"Can't do this." My stiff neck managed a short shake, and I held up my hand to stop her approach. "P-please, stop t-talking."

Sarah's lips parted with a gasp. I'd heard it too. My stutter—the one that never happened around her. It was happening, and I couldn't seem to stop it.

"I-I…" Pushing off the wall, I stumbled for my keys. "I've g-gotta g-go." My stomach jerked and spasmed as I tried to speak, fear pulsing through me so strong I couldn't see straight.

"Justin, please." She held out her hand to me.

I whipped my head around to look at her—my lighthouse, my sparkling star.

But all I could see was another man holding her,

running his hands over her porcelain skin, squeezing her, kissing her…making her moan.

Yanking the door open, I tumbled to my car before she could stop me. I tore out of our driveway so fast I nearly hit another car. The driver blasted his horn and swore out the window. I ignored him, swerving the other way and accelerating down the street. I had no idea where I was going or what the hell I was supposed to do when I got there.

I just had to get away from an ugly truth that was set on hammering the final nail into my coffin.

FIFTEEN

SARAH

I cried so much I had to call in sick on Monday morning. I could barely get out of bed. My legs were weak from exhaustion. My face was puffy and tender. Staggering to the bathroom, I relieved myself, digging my elbows into my knees and starting to cry all over again.

Seriously? Even while I was peeing?

I wondered if I'd ever stop.

When Blake died, I had Justin to hold me. He was solid as a rock, stoic and calm throughout the funeral. That night, we lay in bed together. Neither of us could sleep. We just lay there in the darkness, listening to music and holding each other.

Our only communication was a few whispered words—a promise.

Swiping at my tears, I left the bathroom and slumped down the stairs. I didn't know what I was going to do with my day. I hadn't had a day off since we got back to LA. I started work three days after Blake's funeral, and I hadn't stopped since.

The house was quiet, but not in a comfortable way. If anything, I found the silence disconcerting. Heading for the stereo, I pressed Play, not even caring what came on.

"Bulletproof Weeks" by Matt Nathanson started. It was a mournful, slow tune that hurt my heart, but I let it play. Wrapping my bathrobe around myself, I shuffled into the kitchen. I hadn't eaten since throwing up in Vegas. I couldn't imagine ever enjoying food again, but my growling stomach only accentuated how light my head felt.

Reaching into the pantry, I pulled out a packet of graham crackers. I nibbled the corner of one and shuffled across to the coffee machine. I didn't really want to wake up and face my nightmare, but I had to be at work the next day. I had to pull myself together and keep moving. Staying in this lonely house would kill me.

I'd tried calling Justin a few times since he'd taken off, but he had yet to reply. There was nothing I could do but wait it out. Hopefully, he'd come back to me soon.

The front door creaked open. I jumped away from the coffee machine and rushed into the entranceway. Justin eased through the door. His rumpled T-shirt and unshaven face matched his wild curls. Where had he slept? What had he been doing all night? Fear pitched inside me, and I scrambled to put my armor on as I approached him.

Justin's eyes rounded when he saw me, but he didn't linger for long. His expression went bland as he shuffled past me and headed upstairs.

"Justin?"

I raced after him, nearly slipping on the steps. Pressing my hand into the carpet, I scrambled up the last two stairs and rushed into our room.

Justin was standing at our closet, shoving clothes into a large sports bag. His movements were fast and jerky as he punched the clothes into it.

"What are you doing?" My jaw trembled so hard I had to grit my teeth in order to talk.

"I need my stuff." His voice mirrored his face—dispassionate and lifeless.

I shuffled away from the doorframe. "Where are you going?" My voice hitched.

He didn't answer, just kept packing his stupid bag.

My nostrils flared and I moved into his space, snatching the bag off him and throwing it on the floor. "How long will you be gone?"

With a light sigh, he avoided eye contact and calmly picked up the bag. Clearing his throat, he pulled out the last of his pants and pushed them in.

"No." I shook my head, crossing my arms

tightly to hold myself together. "You can't leave me."

He shot me a dry glare before turning for our dresser. Opening the top drawer, he ripped out handfuls of underwear and socks, sprinkling them into his bag like herbs into a pasta sauce.

"Justin, please!"

He flinched at the way I screamed the words. Turning slowly, he gave me a look that forced my eyes to the floor.

"Why'd you tell me?" His whisper came out broken and weak.

My lips bunched together, my eyes filling with tears. My voice was a quaking mess when I spoke. "Because I need to fix this. I didn't want anything between us. If I'd kept it a secret, I was scared you'd find out and I'd lose you. I want to be honest. Please, we need to work this out."

"How?" he spat, zipping up his bag. The sound shot through the room with a finality that hurt. "Sarah, I can't even look at you."

His words were a punch to the chest. My jaw worked to the side as I fought for air. Finally, I managed to whisper, "But...I didn't mean to." I shuddered. "Justin, I love you."

"Really?" His skeptical tone slapped me in the face.

I blinked, my neck feeling weak and rubbery as I tipped my head. "You know I do."

His face bunched with an angry scowl, and he threw his bag on the floor before running his hands through his reckless curls.

"I can't stop thinking about some other guy inside you." His voice was thick and ragged. "It's tortured me all night. I can't..." Pressing his lips together, he looked to the ceiling and shook his head. "We'd only ever been with each other. You were mine, Sarah...and now some other guy's had you. How do I move past that?"

I shuffled closer to him, hating the distance between us. "I know it's going to be hard, but you need to trust in my love for you. You need to forgive me."

His expression softened for a fleeting moment, giving me hope.

But then his words killed it.

"I want to, but I don't know if I can."

My forehead wrinkled. Desperation made my voice high and shaky when I pointed at him. "You made me a promise, Justin Doyle."

"So did you," he clipped, snatching his bag off the floor. "And you broke yours."

I had no comeback. All I could do was slump against the wall and watch him leave me. The second the front door clicked shut, I slid to the carpet and drew my knees to my chin. Clutching my legs, I tried to hold my shaking body together. Tears burned my aching eyes, but they didn't fall. They would eventually, I was sure of it. I was caught in the middle of a raging ocean, and I didn't have a life jacket anymore. The tears would come. They'd fill up every inch of me until I was drowning in them.

SIXTEEN

JUSTIN

I slapped the file closed and shoved it to the side of my desk. Work had been going well this week, although still piled high around me—because it was the only thing keeping me sane—I was getting it done.

Clay signed off on the latest contract negotiations that morning. All that was left to do was set up a meeting with Marcus and the new band. By next week, signatures would be marking pages and I could move on to something less stressful. Hopefully. If Everett didn't dump more stuff on me as soon as he got back from Bora Bora.

Marcus had popped in to check on me earlier, telling me I should go home to be with my wife. His perceptive gaze and innocent questions unnerved me, but I pushed thoughts of Sarah aside and pulled my law textbook out. I had an exam the next day, and I was behind on my studying. Squinting at the fine text, I reread the paragraph I'd started in the early hours of the morning.

Sleep had been evading me. I felt like a robot fueled by caffeine and the obsessive need to plod forward consistently enough that I didn't have to stop and face my pain. My batteries could never be fully recharged, because every time I closed my eyes I pictured my wife writhing under someone else. Was he tall? Muscly? Handsome?

Would she ever see him again?

I did and did *not* want to know the answers to those questions. They burned inside me though—a red flag waving in front of my eyes. But if I found out the answers, what would that do to me?

What if I knew him?

What if I'd shaken his hand?

I'd never been to after-work drinks with Sarah, but I'd briefly met a couple of her designer friends. Was it Jules? Had he had my wife at The Venetian in Vegas?

Sarah said he was gay, but what if his effeminate hand flicks were just a ruse? What if they'd secretly been doing it for months and finally Sarah couldn't hold it in any longer?

The pen in my hand snapped, making me jerk and hiss at the same time. The sharp plastic nicked my skin. I sucked the blood and threw the broken pen into the trash can under my desk. Rubbing the wound, I gazed at the small red cut, and once again found myself swamped by that overwhelming realization that I was alone.

I'd walked out on my wife.

What the hell was I supposed to do now?

A sharp tap on my door made me look up. Everett Torrence strode in, a half smile tugging his mouth up at the corner. "Afternoon, son."

"H-hi."

"I just wanted to stop by and congratulate you. Clay said you've done a great job on the contract."

"Th-thank you, sir."

Everett filled up most of the chair when he took a seat opposite me. His large, intimidating body made me sit back. Placing my hands on my lap, I rubbed my cut and hoped my expression was calm and neutral.

"So, Adeline wanted me to invite you and Sarah over for dinner...when we get back from our vacation, of course." He chuckled.

I let out a nervous laugh that sounded more like a mouse squeaking.

Clearing my throat, I pulled back my shoulders and tried to go for mature and manly. "You must be looking forward to your v-v-vacation."

"We sure are." He grinned. "It'll be nice to get away for a few days." He pointed at me. "But we want to have a decent catch-up when we return. Feels like we haven't seen you two in a really long time." His jacket hitched at the shoulder when he shrugged.

I shifted in my seat, clearing my throat again to delay my answer. A sick fear twisted my stomach into knots. How was I supposed to reply? I couldn't tell him the truth. Sarah may have hurt me, but I wasn't about to dump her in it. Besides, what did her betrayal say about me?

"We're b-both pretty swamped with w-work at the m-moment, but I-I-I can a-ask her."

"It won't be for at least a week. I'm sure you can fit us in."

I gave him a tight smile.

Everett leaned forward with a sigh, resting his elbows on his knees and staring straight at me. "I know it's been a tough year for you two. Marriage, new house, new jobs…not to mention the loss of your brother."

My throat grew thick and gummy when I tried to swallow.

"But you two are gonna make it. You've both got great work ethic. Now is the time in your life that you really want to make inroads for your future, you know? If you can get this law degree, learn everything you can from Clay and me, then you're going to set yourselves up great. Do it before a family comes along, that's what I say. You work hard in these early years, then you're going to be able to whisk Sarah away for the island getaways she deserves."

I nodded, gripping the arm of my chair and trying to keep it all in.

"Anyway, talk to my daughter and we'll work

out a time to have a meal together." He shot out of his chair and made for the door.

Relief whistled through me but then evaporated when he turned back and asked, "Oh, by the way, how was Sarah's show in Vegas?"

"G-great."

"I didn't know about it until Adeline told me yesterday. You should have mentioned that's where you needed to be this weekend."

"I-I didn't want to l-let you down, sir."

Everett grinned and wagged his finger at me. "That's a good man. Keep the father-in-law happy." He barked out a loud laugh then shook his head. "But seriously, family first, son. Next time your wife asks you to be at one of her fashion shows, you make sure to be there."

Sick bile swirled in my stomach when I tried to smile at him.

"I can't tell you how proud I am of my little girl. The rate she's going, she'll be a celebrity in her own right. You're a lucky man, Justin." The pointed look he gave me before turning and walking away said more than his words ever could.

You look after my baby girl, or I'm going to finish you.

I rested my head on the back of my chair and looked up to the ceiling with a miserable sigh. I wondered how proud he'd be if he knew what his precious little girl got up to in Vegas.

"He'd no doubt find some way to blame me," I muttered.

I'd never been good enough for his daughter.

Scrubbing a hand over my face, I forced myself to sit back up and stare at my law book again. Self-loathing would have me for dinner if I didn't concentrate on something else. I had no idea how Sarah and I would get out of having a meal with her parents. That problem seemed too big to face in that moment, so I focused back on the tiny text in the mammoth book and drowned myself in a sea of law. It was boring. It was mind-numbing. But it was safe.

SEVENTEEN

SARAH

I only took Monday off. Tuesday morning, I had to drag my exhausted butt to the Echelon Fashion building, puffy eyes and all. I walked into the old-style brick factory that had been refitted into a chic, modern workspace. Open-floor planning, which I initially thought was so amazing and cool, turned into another burden. People were constantly moving around—dancing and humming as they worked on their designs, popping past my station with ideas and questions. Jules worked right next to me, his dark eyes like laser beams every time he flashed me a concerned smile.

A thick layer of makeup hid the brunt of my pain. I stayed near my desk and kept my head down. Thankfully, there was a lot to do, and most people were caught in the throes of prepping for Paris.

With Vegas behind us, we were gearing up for our European tour. Enrique liked to put a fresh twist on his Euro-line, so new designs and variations of what we showed in Vegas were expected by the time he returned from New York. Thank God he was in New York. I didn't want to face him. The man had the keenest eyes in the world; he could strip anyone bare with only a look.

My excuse that I was battling some kind of virus probably wouldn't fly with him.

I flicked out the shirt I was working on and held it up to the light. The sheer cream fabric would float and sway around the model perfectly with the cut I'd chosen. I wanted to give it a little something more. It was stunning now, but it needed an edge.

Pre-Vegas, I would have come up with one in a snap. But my creative light was swamped by a foggy sorrow. I couldn't seem to think past the basics.

I dropped the shirt to my table with a heavy sigh and snatched my sketch book from the shelf underneath. Flipping it open, I thumbed through the pages, looking for my original design concepts…the ones I came up with *before* Vegas.

Damn Vegas.

I felt like everything I did revolved around that cursed word. I had been so excited to go—to explore, to celebrate…to rekindle.

But all I'd done was hurt the person I loved most.

The pages nearly ripped as I flicked through them, my movements growing fast and agitated the more I relived waking up next to the wrong man. With a frustrated huff, I slapped the book closed and smacked my hand on the cover.

I should have quit the day I got back.

I couldn't do the job anymore. I couldn't focus. I didn't want to interact with anyone, and I sure as hell didn't want to bump into *him* again. What would I do when he walked into the office? He traveled a lot—New York, Milan, London…Vegas. The guy could show up to the LA offices at a moment's notice.

My fingers shook as I pressed them to my forehead.

But what would I do if I quit?

Justin had left me. I needed a source of income to keep me afloat while we waded through this crap. There was no way on Earth I could tell my parents what I'd done. I had to keep my mouth shut, my head down…and get on with life. Justin would come around eventually, right?

My eyes smarted and I covered my mouth, tears blurring my vision.

"Please come around," I whispered against my palm.

It'd been less than a week. We'd spoken once since he collected his stuff and left. I called so many times on Monday night that eventually he answered and begged me to please give him some space to think. I hadn't had the guts to call him again.

And so I was playing this cruel waiting game.

I missed him.

The house was cold and empty without him.

I dreaded going home each night, but I didn't want to stay at work either. The only thing distracting me from my nightmare was trying to get through the workload piling up around me. But I couldn't work fast enough. My creative juices had dried up. The well inside me that usually bubbled over was nothing more than a dribble.

Sniffing at my tears, I reached for a tissue and found Julian's gaze on me again.

I shook my head then dabbed at my eyes. "Please don't ask, Jules. I can't talk about it."

"I'm here if you need me, *chica*." He moved around his table and came to stand in front of me. Resting his elegant hands against the wood, he gave me his best smile.

He was so gorgeous with his dark skin and wide brown eyes. He was dressed in a bright purple shirt with a floral print collar and a pair of pinstriped pants that hugged his slender figure perfectly. He always dressed with flair. I loved that about him.

The gold ring on his pinky finger caught the light as he waved his hand in the air. "Jules always has a hug available for you, pretty blue eyes."

I sniffed again, attempting a smile. It didn't work. I couldn't lift my quivering lips past a half-assed twitch.

Grabbing the shirt I was working on, I clutched the floating fabric and shook it in the air. "I just can't seem to get this right. I know it needs something more, but what? I can't come up with anything today!"

"This week," Jules murmured with a knowing smile. His full lips pursed as his eyes traveled over my breasts then down to my belly. "You're not pregnant, are you?"

Fear spiked my chest like an ice-cold dagger. My eyes popped so wide they actually hurt. I hadn't even thought about that. It couldn't…

The idea was so horrifying that bile surged up my throat. I slapped my hand over my mouth and ran for the bathroom. Shoving the door open, I nearly took out Jenna. She yelped and jumped out of my way, but I didn't have time to apologize. All I could do was smack open a stall door and lunge for the bowl. My stomach hadn't been very full, so once my banana smoothie was out, it became kind of painful. My stomach kept jerking and heaving though, driven by a blinding terror that I might be knocked up.

No, I couldn't. This could not happen.

I always used protection.

Squeezing my eyes shut, I retched up a little bile before slumping to the floor and heaving in some oxygen. Had I used protection in Vegas?

My stomach shuddered, threatening another violent attack. I lurched up to my knees and gripped the porcelain, but nothing came. I was scrambling for a memory of the night, some kind of indication that we'd been safe, but I couldn't conjure it. Until that point, I'd been grateful I couldn't remember much. I didn't want to relive my shame. I didn't want to understand how I could have let myself do something so awful.

But…

"No, please, no," I whimpered. "I can't be pregnant."

How did I find out? It'd only happened six days ago. Did the body know that fast? I tried to figure out when my period was due but couldn't think past the word: *PREGNANT.* My sisters talked about ovulation when they were trying to start their families. I'd listened with half an ear as they discussed the optimal timing for conception. Had I been in that window? I'd barely listened to those conversations. Kids weren't even on my radar.

The idea of taking a pregnancy test made me shiver.

"Sarah, sweetie, are you okay?" Jules called through the bathroom door.

I couldn't form any kind of coherent sentence so I just whined in my throat.

The door creaked open, and his polished shoes clicked across the tiled floor. I hadn't bothered to lock the stall. He found me easily.

With a sigh, he bent down and helped me up. Only Jules would walk into a ladies' room to collect some hurling wretch off the floor. Guiding me to the basin, he pulled some paper towels free and wet them. I dabbed my face, attempting to clean up the makeup massacre on my cheeks.

"So, pregnant?" He crossed his arms, his right eyebrow peaked.

"I can't be." I shook my head vehemently.

He snickered. "Why not?"

Because Justin and I haven't had sex in months, which means the father would have to be...

The thought was so abhorrent, I nearly ran for the stall again. But after a painful jerk, my stomach settled. Gazing into the mirror, I stared at my pasty white complexion. A year ago, I'd been beautiful, filled with light and joy. Now everything was broken, and I looked like a wide-eyed urchin.

Tears swamped my vision, turning the mirror into a warped piece of glass. My chin began to tremble.

"Oh, *chica*." Jules pulled me into his arms, resting my head on his shoulder and holding me tight.

I wrapped my arms around him, clinging to his shirt and praying for an empty womb.

I'd never win Justin back with another man's baby growing inside me.

EIGHTEEN

JUSTIN

The examination room was suffocating. The only noise I could hear was the ticking clock on the wall and the scratch of pen on paper. Except for my pen.

My pen was doing fuck all.

I wriggled the Biro and glared down at the question. I didn't know what kind of answer they were looking for. I'd spent the week cramming study into my spare time, and it'd all flown out my ears the second I sat down.

I couldn't think past Sarah. A blonde with a physique just like my wife's had taken a seat two rows in front of me. That was it. I was done.

Closing my eyes, I scraped my fingers through my hair and bit my tongue against the string of swear words I wanted to unleash.

I wished Blake was there. He always knew the right thing to say.

He'd slap my shoulder, giving it a squeeze as he imparted some insight I hadn't thought to consider. His take on Sarah's dirty deeds in Vegas would have been interesting.

Shit! I wanted him back.

I wanted to sit down with a cold beer and just shoot the breeze with him. I wanted to play a game of pool and share my woes while the balls fired across the green table. We used to tell each other everything around a pool table. The hours we spent in our basement in Albuquerque—laughing, chatting, hanging out. Secrets were shared and revealed, our bond solidified.

I wanted my brother. I *needed* him.

But he wasn't there. Damn it, why hadn't he worn a helmet? Why had he sent me off to check on his wife? If he hadn't been recklessly driving on the wrong side of the road, none of this shit would have happened. Sarah wouldn't have gone to Vegas alone and ended up cheating on me!

I snapped my eyes shut, my bitter blaming working like razor blades on my conscience. How could I even think that? Blaming a dead guy—that was a new low.

My throat constricted, cutting off my air supply until a thumping headache threatened to blind me.

Images of Blake's broken body shot through my mind. They were still crystal clear, like a photograph I could never throw into the fire. Dad and I had rushed to the scene while Sarah comforted a shell-shocked Jane. We hadn't spoken as we tore along the country roads.

Dad slammed on the brakes when we spotted the flashing lights.

A red sedan was sticking awkwardly out of the ditch. Workers gathered around the front of the car. I caught a glimpse of blond hair, matted with blood. Arms bent at funny angles, combined with the quiet murmur of voices around her, told me the female driver hadn't survived the crash either.

I shuddered, my stomach vibrating as I ran around the police officers and spotted my brother's mangled bike.

"Justin." Dad's brother, the one who'd called in the accident, clutched me against him, trying to face me away from the wreck. I wrestled him off me, shoving him back so I could get access to my brother.

"Blake!" I screamed, running for the ditch.

Uncle Jack nearly tore my jacket trying to stop me. I surged forward, slipping down the shallow embankment until I stood in a small puddle of water and came face to face with my brother. Dark red blood painted his pale white forehead. It oozed from the gruesome wound tearing his skull apart. It looked like someone had taken a mace to his head, smashing it into his skull until a deep indent had formed.

I crumpled to my knees, my pinstriped pants sinking into the mud. I couldn't take my eyes off Blake. He stared back at me, his pale brown gaze void of life.

"Oy! Get them back!" a British voice boomed. "Sir! Excuse me, sir! You need to move away. Sir!"

I couldn't respond. I could barely move.

My chest heaved with disbelief as I knelt in that mud, trying to convince myself that it was all just a bad dream.

We flew Blake's crumpled body home. The funeral was the worst day of my life. I couldn't get Blake's dead gaze out of my mind. My parents became obsessed with knowing details of the accident—who was to blame, how it had even occurred.

I didn't want to know.

It wouldn't bring Blake home.

I'd heard some murmurings one night about faults being on both sides. My mother was arguing with Dad about the reckless woman driving too fast, while Dad countered with the fact Blake wasn't wearing a helmet and he'd accidentally veered onto the wrong side of the road.

"He wouldn't do that!"

"It was his wedding day! And he was driving on the opposite side to normal. Esther, it would have been the easiest mistake in the world."

"Oh, just shut up, Carson! I can't talk about this!" She'd stormed from the room and slammed every door along the way.

That was how my parents had dealt with the loss—anger and tears. We'd visited them in Albuquerque for Christmas, and they'd seemed to have calmed down a little. They were finding their way…unlike Sarah and me.

We hadn't yelled at each other once.

We'd taken the silent route to recovery. Thing was, recovery had never happened. People always say time's the best healer.

People were full of shit.

Gritting my teeth, I tried to reread the question. I'd be getting a call from Mom later. Without Blake around, she'd turned all her attention to me and my achievements. I had to fill the void her eldest son had left behind. I'd become the one who had to make the family proud.

My insides quaked as I imagined telling them about my failed marriage. I couldn't do it. How would I even form the words?

Yeah, Mom, hey, so my wife cheated on me.

She probably wouldn't even be surprised. Sarah had always been too good for me. Her father thought so. Hell, everyone probably did. They just didn't have the guts to come out and say it.

Since Sarah had slept with someone else, I was even more worthless.

Before, she didn't have anyone to compare me with.

I let out a brittle snicker and shook my head. The guy had probably been a fucking stallion, giving her all the pleasure she deserved. Unlike me. The guy who pounded her so hard she'd cried out in pain.

Making a fist, I thumped my exam paper.

Everyone around me jumped. The proctor

glared at me, making the *shh* symbol with her finger to her lips. I looked away then shook my head.

I couldn't do this.

Jerking out of my chair, I snatched the paper and marched to the front of the room. I still had ninety minutes left to complete the test, but I slapped my unfinished work on the main table and walked out.

Who gave a rat's ass about law anyway?

I was about to lose my wife. Failing an exam was nothing.

Swinging the door back, I marched out of the room and set out to do something that would be the end of me. But I had to.

It wasn't fair to string Sarah along.

I had to set her free.

NINETEEN

SARAH

It'd been a week. Seven soulless nights since I'd torn a hole through my marriage. I spent the weekend shut up in the house. I switched off my phone and drowned in a sea of mournful music.

"Hello" by Adele lapped against me as I lay on the couch and stared at the blank TV screen. I blinked slowly, wondering if I'd ever find the courage to call Justin and apologize again. Rubbing a hand over my stomach, I clutched his loose T-shirt—the one I'd taken from his drawer the night he left. It'd become my favorite nightshirt, and I never wanted to take it off again. It was stained with tears and snot, but I didn't want to wash it. I didn't want to lose his smell. Lifting it to my nose, I inhaled his masculine scent and closed my eyes.

As much as I wanted to call him, I couldn't.

I still didn't know if I was pregnant or not. I took a test and it came up negative, but these things weren't always accurate. My sister had taken a test that came up negative, and a few days later she was positive. She'd just taken the test too early. I didn't have the courage to take another one. Fear still pulsed through me. I'd always suffered from irregular periods, so I had a vague idea of when it was due, but no certainty. Did that make my chances of getting pregnant less or more?

How the hell did I know! I didn't want to spend hours researching on the Internet. Terror had shut down all my senses, and I was nothing more than a beached whale, lying on my couch and listening…

Listening to songs that were turning my heart to useless specks of ash.

Joan Osborne's version of "Ain't No Sunshine" started to play and I rolled away from it, gripping the cushion under my chin and curling into a ball. The ring Justin gave me when he proposed dug into my chin. I pulled back to gaze at the ceylonese sapphire sandwiched by two small solitaires. The stone was a pale, bright blue that matched my eyes. That was what Justin had said anyway. The way he'd smiled at me when he slipped the ring onto my finger. And his proposal. Oh, man, his perfect proposal.

I sucked in a ragged breath and sniffed against

the tears. The song soaked into my back, taunting me with questions. Was this my life now? A sunless, lonely room?

I shuddered and bit my bottom lip, trying to stop the quivering.

The ringing doorbell made me jerk. I gasped and bolted upright, gripping the couch with wide eyes.

"Justin?" I whispered, throwing off the blanket and lurching for the door. The blanket wrapped around my knees, tripping me up. I thumped onto the wood floor. "Shit. Coming! I'm coming!"

I didn't want him changing his mind and taking off before I could talk to him.

Wrestling out of the blanket was like waging a war with a sea monster. I kicked and bucked but didn't manage to unhinge myself completely until a few steps before the door. Tossing it aside with an angry huff, I brushed the hair off my face and stopped to take in a breath.

It wasn't until I was reaching for the handle that it occurred to me—this was Justin's house too. He didn't need to ring the doorbell. My hopeful smile morphed into a frown as I yanked the door open to find my best friend gazing at me with a bemused smile.

Her eyebrows popped high as she took in my sloppy appearance.

"Wow. No offense, but you've looked better. Are you sick?"

I stepped aside to let Jane in. She brushed past me, dumping her handbag in the basket by the door and dropping her keys on the table. She looked around the house on her way to the kitchen.

"I'm in desperate need of a tea. Do you want one?"

"Sure," I mumbled, crossing my arms and shuffling after her.

I should have been happy to see Jane so upbeat. Blake's death had pretty much ruined her. I'd tried to be the best friend I could, but I was dealing with an emotionless robot and it was kind of challenging. We were all in shock, trying to understand how something so unfair could have happened. Widowed on her wedding day. That sort of thing should be reserved for nightmares and horror movies.

Technically, she wasn't a widow, but she and Blake had been sharing a bed since their sophomore year in college. Their wedding day had actually been their five-year "first kiss" anniversary. Way to shit all over a happy memory, right?

The kettle whistled. Jane snatched it off the stand and poured boiling water into each mug.

She glanced over her shoulder at me, her pale brown eyebrows rising. "Seriously, are you sick? Or do you just have your period?"

I swallowed, stark fear scraping through me as I shook my head.

"Just had a rough week," I muttered before turning away from her and slumping into a chair.

Jane carried the mugs over and placed them on the dining room table. Sitting adjacent to me, she carefully studied my pale complexion while quietly steeping her tea.

A year ago, we would have been chattering away like magpies. Death had killed us both, like a silent gas that had been swirling around us, eating our joy, chipping away at our personalities.

Wrapping cold fingers around my mug, I lifted it to my lips and blew on the hot liquid.

"Sorry I haven't been by in a few weeks. The end of the school year is always so crazy, but my students left on Friday and I'm free of pubescent tweens for a while." Jane's voice was so flat and wooden. Would I ever hear her sing again? Laugh?

Hell, she barely cried.

I guess I understood it better now. Having lived without Justin for a week, I finally caught a glimpse of what she went through every night she slipped into an empty bed with no promise of waking up beside her man.

Robot mode was easier—the safest bet.

I attempted a smile, but only managed a fleeting, closed-mouth grin. "I've been busy too. Work is crazy."

"Vegas go okay?" Jane sipped her tea, and I lost the ability to speak.

My head bobbed.

"Really? I know you were nervous."

"It was good," I clipped. "Great show. People loved it."

"And the big boss?"

I clenched my jaw. "Mmhmm, he was very impressed."

"Well done, you." Her lips curved up at the

edges, the closest to a smile anyone got these days.

She reached for my hand and gave it a squeeze. "So, what's next then?"

"Paris," I whispered. "I'm not sure if I'll be invited to go, but hopefully some of my designs will be on the catwalk." I scratched my cheek and rolled my eyes. "If I can get my shit together and actually finish them."

Jane tipped her head. "Of course you will. You're Sarah Doyle. You're the most talented designer I know."

Hearing my married name made my eyes glass with tears.

Jane sat back and pointed at me. "Okay, if you don't have your period yet, it's definitely brewing. You are seriously emotional today."

I sniffed and swiped at my tears. "I'm just…" I shook my head. "Rough week."

Her eyebrows dipped together, and I knew my number was up. I'd never been able to lie to Jane. We were born to be besties. We may have not met until my freshman year at college, but the speed with which we clicked was a testament to how close we'd always be.

I clung to that truth as I drew in a ragged breath then spilled the beans. "I screwed up, Jane. Justin's left me."

Jane choked on her tea, spurting it back into her cup before slamming the mug down on the table. She snatched a tissue from the box in the middle and wiped her mouth before regaining her composure enough to sputter, "What?" Her bottom lip was slack as her green eyes flashed with worry. "He'd never do that. What's going on?"

So, I had to tell her.

Every little detail…at least the ones I could remember. It was like I left my body while I talked. I couldn't recall the exact words I used or how I sold it, but I must have come off looking pretty bad because before I'd even finished, she lurched out of her chair so fast it fell backward, scarring my parents' wooden floor.

She didn't apologize. She was too busy huffing like a dragon and glaring at me. Her thin chest heaved while she bunched her long fingers into fists. The emerald engagement ring Blake had given her looked massive against her white knuckles. I wondered how long it would take for her to remove it. I glanced at my ring and figured…a hell of a long time.

"How could you?" Jane's voice shook.

I closed my eyes and dipped my head, summoning the courage to look back up at the dragon. "I didn't mean—"

"You *have* a husband! You *have* everything I want! And you just throw it away?" She threw her hands wide. "What is wrong with you?" This was the most emotional I'd seen her since Blake's funeral. Her pale cheeks were burning red, her green eyes vibrant with disgust.

"I was drunk," I punched out. "I didn't know what I was doing."

"I don't understand how you could let something like this happen! You're blaming

alcohol? Give me a break, Sarah! You disgust me."
She spat the words at my head, towering over me
with her fiery red hair and wild eyes.

I deserved it. I disgusted myself. If Jane had ever
cheated on Blake, I would have taken her to the
cleaners.

As much as I wanted her support, I couldn't
expect it. So I just sat there and let her stare at me
like I was the world's biggest tramp.

"Justin's a good man."

"The best." My face bunched as I choked out the
words.

"You don't deserve him." Her voice was deep
and metallic, made even more brutal by the
thumping of her feet as she marched for the door.

I stayed where I was, staring ahead as I
identified each sound—the flick of the doorknob,
the snatching of the keys, the hitching of the
handbag, and then the harrowing door slam that
made me flinch.

The music had stopped playing while Jane
visited, and now all that remained was a thick,
gloomy silence.

I sat in it—small and alone at my dining room
table. I had no motivation to get up or do anything
other than blink and stare at the upturned chair
and the uneven groove scarring the polished floor.

TWENTY

JUSTIN

It was dark out. I'd had a shitty Saturday visiting the courthouse and finding out what I had to do. Hours online researching and downloading documents put me in a foul mood. By Sunday, I could do nothing more than sit on my stale motel bed and stare at my computer screen.

Images of Blake's and Jane's smiling faces filled the space. They were a mix of live action and still shots. "I Love You Always Forever" played in the background of the wedding video I'd made them. I had planned to use it as part of my best man speech. While Sarah had stayed up in the early hours making Jane's dress, I'd hunched over my computer, cutting, editing, splicing until I'd created the perfect four-minute video for them.

I'd chosen one of Jane's favorite Donna Lewis songs to accompany the collage of their life together. Sarah had swooned when I played it to her, sitting on my lap with her slender arm around my shoulders.

"You're so amazing," she'd whispered, her eyes sparkling as she watched the screen.

I'd loved doing that. Editing, creating beautiful images like that made me so incredibly happy. I'd been doing it ever since I was a kid, taking photos and video clips of any and everything. Turning them into mini-movies. We'd watch them on the weekends sometimes, or I'd make a special one for family occasions like Christmas and Thanksgiving.

Blake had tried to convince me to pursue it in college, but my parents were pushing law so hard it was easier to keep my technical talents as a hobby.

Making video clips for fun won't set you up financially, son. You need to get yourself a decent career first.

My dad had made a good point, and I followed his advice. It was just easier than putting up a fight. After I met Sarah and she'd trusted me enough to divulge her wedding business dreams, I'd had even more reason to pursue a stable career that could support her.

Everything had fallen into place so easily—our lives mapped out for us by everyone who cared.

It'd been simpler to let people take charge. We'd been so happy together we hadn't even noticed it happening around us.

Where had that left me?

In a job I hated, working like a dog to please the people I loved.

And I was fucking miserable.

I double-clicked on the next clip in my folder. Blake's smile hit me first. It was vivid and eye-catching. He winked at the camera and pointed. "You ready, bro?"

"Yeah, go for it."

He shifted in his chair, resting the guitar on his knee and tucking a long curl behind his ear before starting to strum.

I panned the camera to the door. I remembered the way my heart kicked when Jane and Sarah slipped into the room.

"What's going on?" Jane barely had time to ask her question before Blake started playing "The Book of Love."

Her lips parted when he started singing. Her eyes misted over. Blake's voice stretched across the room, drawing her toward him. I followed her slow steps, zooming in on her face while she basked in the glow of Blake's love.

Nestling at his feet, she rested her long fingers on his faded jeans while he sang to her. A couple of tears tracked down her cheeks as he came to the end of the song then softly whispered, "Wanna marry me, Janey?"

She giggled. "You know it."

I caught Sarah's eyes on me through the camera lens. They were sparkling like sapphires, telling me she loved me.

I touched my computer screen, running my finger over her face. Had she known then that my proposal was in the pipeline? Had she known then that, only two and half years after I shot that clip, she'd be standing by Blake's graveside, trying to comfort a girl who'd lost the love of her life?

If only we'd been able to see into the future back then. I would have stopped Blake from playing that song. I would have told him to just live with Jane for the rest of his life, to never fly to England and get married in a beautiful stone church.

If I'd known what was going to transpire, I never would have approached Sarah that first night I saw her.

I expected the thought to maybe bring me a small sense of comfort. But it didn't. Because if I hadn't spoken to her that night, I never would have known what it was to love her.

And at college, I was convinced that loving her made me a better man.

It was still true.

She'd always brought out the best in me. Blake's death had severed something inside, cut off my ability to let Sarah in. So she'd gone somewhere else…and she'd had every right to.

I needed to let her go. We both needed to move on.

I had no idea what moving on looked like, but I didn't think I could stomach law or Torrence

Records for much longer. Slapping my laptop closed, I pushed it off my legs and stared across the darkened room.

Without Sarah, none of that stuff was worth it.

I just had to stay long enough to get things finalized, have a little money in my pocket, make sure she was financially secure as well, and then I could quit and move on.

It was time I left my life behind and stopped trying to live up to everybody else's expectations. For the first time ever, I could figure out what the hell I wanted.

TWENTY-ONE

SARAH

The restaurant felt cluttered and nauseating. The smell of rich Italian meat sauce was churning my stomach, making me want to run to the toilet and throw up. Reaching for my water glass, I downed the clear liquid then patted my mouth with the cloth napkin.

Maria rotated her fork in her spaghetti, using her spoon to make a neat mound that would fit into her mouth. My nose crinkled as I watched her suck up a loose strand then start munching.

"You not hungry?" Libby touched my arm.

Her cold fingers made me flinch. I gazed down

at my half-eaten lasagna and shook my head.

"Well, at least have some wine." She lifted the bottle and went to pour me some, but I smacked my hand over my glass before she could.

"No, thanks," I clipped.

"You're not drinking either?" Maria's pale eyebrows made a sharp V. "What is up with you today?"

"I just don't feel like drinking." I shrugged. "I have a busy day at work and…"

I never want to touch alcohol again, because it makes you forget and do stupid things that ruin your life.

"Oh, no way." Maria's fork clattered into her bolognese bowl. "I told you to wait."

"What are you talking about?" Libby frowned at her.

I stared at the empty chair in front of me, so grateful my mother was away in Bora Bora. I didn't want her witnessing my demise. I knew exactly what Maria was getting at, and I didn't know if I had the power to refute her. Because I still didn't know if I was pregnant or not.

"Sparky's pregnant." Maria announced it like a fact, while I shuddered in my seat.

"No, I'm not." My argument sounded so lame and pathetic.

Libby's eyes narrowed in on my face.

I hated these damn monthly lunches. I needed to figure a way out of them.

"You're kind of acting like you might be pregnant." Libby's voice was soft and genteel.

I met her sweet tone with a sharp snap. "Or my

period might be brewing."

Slapping the napkin down on top of my cutlery, I huffed and crossed my arms.

"Something's brewing," Maria muttered, bulging her eyes and slurping up another noodle.

Libby snickered. Glancing at Mom's empty spot, she no doubt wished our matriarch were there. I scowled at her then shot a glare at Maria when she asked, "So, come on then. Spill."

"I don't have anything to spill." I flicked my hands in the air. "Why can't I just be having a really shitty day?"

Libby's eyes popped wide, her head jolting back.

"You guys have them all the time, and I have to sit here listening to you bitch and moan about the trials of motherhood and trying to run a busy household. But no, I have to be perfect, right? The youngest. Apple of Daddy's eye. The sweet little golden girl who never does anything wrong. I'm not allowed to get a little pissy when things don't go my way?"

"Sweetie." Libby reached for me again, but I tucked my arm beneath the table before she could touch me. "What's not going your way?"

"Nothing!" I slumped back in my seat and looked up to the ceiling. My heart was racing so fast I thought I was going to pass out. No way in hell was I telling them the truth. Clenching my jaw, I jerked back up and muttered, "I'm just under a lot of pressure at work and I'm tired."

"Well, is there anything we can do to help?"

Maria leaned toward me on the other side and I felt completely boxed in.

Maybe I could crawl under the table and bolt for the door. I'd never get away with that though. I had to pull it together or fess up. And fessing up to my sisters was never going to happen.

Sniffing in a sharp breath, I raised my hands and gently pushed them away from me. "I'm just having a little outburst. All I want to do is rant and complain for a second, and then I'll be fine. In fact, I'm already feeling better."

Maria's left eyebrow peaked and her lips bunched as she tried to quell her laughter.

"What?" I swatted her arm.

"That's it? You're already feeling better? Come on, that rant was, like, less than thirty seconds. Girl, you seriously have some work to do."

"Yeah, I mean, when I get going, I can be fuming for a good half hour." Libby grinned. "Poor Trent." She shook her head and squeezed my shoulder. "Justin's a really lucky guy if you're only a thirty-second ranter."

I frowned and shrugged my sister's hand off me.

Maria snorted. "I remember when I was pregnant, poor Lyle would just sit there on the couch, watching me pace and cry, my big fat belly poking out." She laughed. "He'd look at me with this kind of glazed, gobsmacked expression, tracking me back and forth across the room. He always knew not to come in with the hug until I'd finished with my 'I'm a whale' cry."

Libby laughed, rocking back in her chair as she

covered her mouth. I forced out a chuckle, wondering who would listen to me as I paced around my living room, fat, alone, and pregnant.

The thought worked like an electric shot to jolt me out of my seat. I gripped the edge of the table to steady myself, while my sisters both looked at me like I'd just slapped them awake.

"Sorry," I snickered. "I just have to go to the bathroom."

They nodded then turned back to each other, sharing a curious look before Libby launched into her own pregnancy story.

I rested my hand over my belly, clutching my blouse as I double-timed it to the bathroom. I didn't know if I wanted to hurl or pee. My bladder stepped up as I pushed the stall door open and I pulled down my pants. Lowering myself on shaky legs, I rested my elbows on my knees and spotted my salvation.

With a gasp, I tugged at my underwear, taking a closer look at the spots of blood. So familiar. So comforting.

"Oh, thank you, God." My voice jumped and quaked over the words. Gripping my mouth, I released a dry sob that could have been either a cry or a laugh...probably a mix.

Who knew that a little blood could give a girl so much hope?

Closing my eyes, I let a lone tear slide down my cheek before cleaning up and heading back out to the restaurant. I snatched the handbag off the back of my chair and immediately excused myself to the bathroom before my sisters could ask any questions.

By the time I did eventually return, they'd both worked out what my little re-run to the ladies' room was all about.

"You know, you should always just take it with you whenever you go anywhere." Maria pointed at my handbag.

I rolled my eyes. "Thanks, Mom."

She giggled and wiped her saucy lips with her napkin.

"So, no kidlet on the way then?"

"No," I sighed. "Thank goodness."

"Really?" Libby looked a little disappointed.

"Lib, come on, my job is insane at the moment. I can't imagine bringing a baby into the mix right now. Maria told me to wait, and I agree with her. A baby's not going to make my life any easier."

"Well, that's true, but…" Libby sighed, her lips rising into a smile that only mothers can give. "They also make life so incredibly beautiful." She touched her chest. "For all my complaints, I love being a mom. My children have made my life complete."

Maria started nodding, her face taking on that affectionate glow as well.

I wanted to slap the table and yell at them. *The only reason it works so great is because you both have loyal husbands to support you. I don't have that anymore! I'm not sure I ever will again!*

The screaming in my brain brought me up short.

No, I couldn't believe that.

I *would* get my husband back.

I wasn't pregnant with another man's child. My chances had jumped from non-existent to slim. Once again, I could shift into the waiting zone and just pray like crazy that after I'd given Justin the space he wanted, he'd come back to me.

Surely he was missing me as much as I was missing him.

Surely the cavity in his chest was growing on a daily basis. Mine definitely was. If he didn't return soon, I couldn't say how much of me there'd be left waiting for him.

TWENTY-TWO

JUSTIN

My briefcase felt heavy as I walked into Torrence Records. I kept my gaze forward as I headed past the main reception. I looked to the ceiling as I stood in the elevator, and I pretended to be checking my phone as I breezed past Kelly and Marcia. They both greeted me, but all I could do was nod.

Slipping into my office, I slapped the case down on my desk and extracted the manila envelope that would change my life. With a heavy sigh, I pulled the divorce papers free and scanned them for what felt like the millionth time.

It'd been time-consuming, yet so straightforward to acquire them. I held the corner and flicked my thumb over the pages. My penmanship was shaky but legible. It took me less than an hour to file them with the courts. All I had left to do was serve them to Sarah, and the process could begin.

Closing my eyes, I reminded myself to breathe. I was doing the right thing. It was a miracle she'd stuck around as long as she had. Blake's death had killed me too. I couldn't be the kind of husband she needed. I couldn't even make love to her anymore.

This divorce would set her free to pursue whomever she wanted.

The idea of Mr. Vegas having her again scorched my stomach. Slamming my teeth together, I forced air through my nose and dropped the divorce papers before my fist could scrunch them.

They floated to the floor around me.

"Oh, here, let me help you." Kelly appeared out of nowhere.

I jerked, surprised I hadn't seen her in my doorway. "N-n-no, that's okay." I dropped to the floor to gather them, but I was too late. She was already crouching down, collecting the sheets.

Her efficient movements ground to a halt when she caught sight of the first page.

"Thanks f-for that." I tried to distract her by snatching it out of her hand, but she lurched away from me. Her eyes were round with despair as she looked up from the pages.

"Please tell me these aren't yours."

I dipped my head and looked down at my desk.

My name is on the first fucking page. Of course it's mine!

I closed my mouth against my sarcastic reply.

Kelly's bright gaze bored into me, her voice firm and unrelenting as she asked, "What's going on?"

"This isn't your concern, K-Kelly." I nestled my hands on my hips but kept my eyes on the floor.

"You haven't even been married a year."

I held out my hand, beckoning for the document with a flick of my fingers. "C-can I have them back, p-please?"

She hugged them to her chest, her eyebrows dipping low. "Not until you tell me what's going on."

"Like I said." I gritted my teeth. "It's not your c-concern."

Her hard expression eased up a little when I looked at her. Maybe she could see how strung out I was. Or did my complete failure just ooze from the pores of my skin these days?

Her tone dropped to a soft lilt. "I don't think you want to do this."

"Oh, yeah?" My breathy laugh was brittle. "H-how do you f-f-figure that?"

"You look like you're about to sign your own death sentence." Her shoulders sagged, the papers slapping against her thigh as she gazed at me.

My face twitched while I tried to rein in my expression. I couldn't let her see how close to the truth she was hitting with that one. "It's for the b-best," I croaked.

"Are you sure? What happened?"

"I c-can't…" I shook my head. "She's better off without me."

Her eyes narrowed. "And you're basing that on what?"

"She chea—" Placing my hands back on my hips, I looked to the ceiling. "I need to l-let her g-go." I cleared my throat, hauling back what little control I had left. "S-some things can't b-be overcome, Kelly. We j-just have to m…" My lips struggled to form the words as my stutter choked me. "Move on," I finally punched out.

Kelly's face crinkled with sadness.

Her expression was killing me, so I snapped my fingers and reached out my hand again. "Give me the p-papers."

She hesitantly passed them back but wouldn't release them until I gave her a sharp frown. "Just be one hundred percent certain before you do this. Marriage is supposed to be forever."

I gazed at her beautiful face. We may have been the same age, but she still had so much to learn.

"Nothing lasts forever." I slapped the papers onto my desk and sniffed. "Now, did you n-need something?"

"Uh…" She sighed. "Yeah, Marcus wants to set up that final contract meeting this afternoon. Are you free?"

"Yep," I clipped. "Just let me know the time as s-soon as you d-do."

"Okay." She paused at my door, resting her elegant fingers on the frame.

I looked away from her and kept my head down, refusing to engage in any more conversation. The only sound in my little office was the shuffling of papers as I reordered my "death sentence" and got ready for my after-work execution.

TWENTY-THREE

SARAH

He was there. Oh, shit, he was in the office.

He'd breezed in from New York about an hour before, with his charming smile and gentle voice. I kept my eyes down, focusing on the dress I was adding a unique thread design to. It had to be hand-stitched, and the intricate pattern took all my concentration.

The average eye wouldn't even notice the fine blend in the material, but this dress was hopefully bound for Paris, and they would most definitely notice it there.

Franco and Jules were chatting with him.

Man, I couldn't even bring myself to think his name.

I didn't want to taste it on my lips again. I couldn't remember if I'd said it sometime during our night together. I mean, I would have uttered it at some point. I just prayed I'd never said it while we were having sex.

My spine did a crazy little twitch. I brushed my cheek on my shoulder, trying to counter the involuntary spasm. I couldn't let him get to me. If I was lucky, he'd only be in for a few days then out the door again. I could do a few days. As long as he didn't talk to me.

"Hello, Sarah." His smooth voice made me flinch.

I looked past his tailored suit and saw Jules grinning at me. He was giving me that excited face—the one that told me good news was coming.

The man unbuttoned his jacket and smoothly slid his hand into his pocket. I glanced up and gave him a tight smile. He was looking over my head at the mannequin behind me.

"The blue dress is looking good. You've made a few adjustments."

I nodded then clipped, "Thank you."

I kept my eyes on the stitch work I was bound to mess up while he stood there. That would go down well…just what I needed.

Pausing, I laid my quivering fingers on the table and looked past his arm, tracking the back of Franco's head as he worked two tables in front of me.

The man leaned down to cross my line of sight. I sniffed and moved back.

Why wasn't he more awkward? How could he stand there looking at me like nothing had happened between us?

"Looks like you might be going to Paris." He grinned. It was a slow crocodile smile that made me twitch.

I tried to respond appropriately. The news should have thrilled me, but all I could do was squeak, "You think so?"

"By the look of that dress, I do."

With a thick swallow, I nodded.

"You're doing so well, Sarah. For such a young designer, you certainly know how to make an impression."

My eyes snapped to his face. It was impossible to miss his double meaning. What an asshole. I hated his triumphant smirk.

My cheeks flamed as I stared down at the dress I was working on, plucking at my waning courage. The guy was my superior. Was it really a good idea to piss him off? I glanced up again. He was still eyeing me, his eyes trailing my torso while he obviously relived our little tryst.

I clenched my fists and quietly asked, "Will, ah… Will you be going?"

His gaze swept over me, the warmth of it doing nothing to improve my mood. I'd liked it once, even appreciated it. Not anymore.

"It's undecided whether I'll be in Paris or not. But I'll be sure to let you know."

He buttoned his jacket again, obviously hoping his charming smile would soften me. Instead, I stiffened, transfixed by the gold ring on his wedding finger.

My nostrils flared as I quietly spat out the words, "Yes, you better do that. Because if you're going, I won't be."

He snickered, my harsh tone surprising him.

"If your designs go, you go. That's the way it works in this company."

"Well…" I tipped my head, no doubt looking like a bird as I tried to be strong without making eye contact. "Well, I'll be pulling my designs if you're going to be there."

I glanced up, making sure he saw how serious I was.

His jaw worked to the side, and he leaned over my workspace with slightly narrowed eyes. "I would advise against that. You don't throw away a chance like Paris."

"Why not?" I whispered. "I've thrown everything else away."

His forehead wrinkled in confusion. I glanced across the open office to make sure no one could hear us before leaning forward and hissing, "You're a married man. How can you stand there looking so smug yet innocent? You cheated on your wife."

"Hmmmm." He stood back, his bottom lip pulling into a thoughtful pout. "It was one night, Sarah. Hardly a love affair. I'm not about to hurt her with the truth. I love her enough to keep our little indiscretion to myself."

I'm not sure what my face did then, but it caused his lips to rise into a pitying smile. It made me feel like pond scum. Was my honesty seriously to blame for Justin leaving me? That wasn't fair! I'd done the right thing, hadn't I?

"Good luck with the rest of your preparations." He nodded, all formal again, like he hadn't been inside me less than two weeks ago. "I hope you make it to Paris."

If anyone else had seen the warm smile he shined me, they'd think he was the world's sweetest guy, wishing me all the best and hoping I made it to Paris so I could advance my career.

What the hell did they know?

The truth was ugly, and maybe it was best kept hidden. Exposing it had only ruined my life. Aside from Justin and Jane, I certainly wouldn't be telling my dirty little secret to anyone else. Maybe I should never have told them...or maybe it would have eaten me alive if I hadn't.

*****

I flicked out the shiny black fabric on my table and pulled it flat. Stepping back, I eyed the square, picturing how it would fall. The scissors were poised in my hand ready to make the big cut.

The office was empty. With a couple of New Yorkers visiting, everyone had gone out for mid-week drinks. I declined. Socializing with work people was the last thing on my radar. If anything,

I despised being around them; it was hard looking people in the eye. Thankfully, everyone had bought into my virus bug fib, but I had to pretend to be better now.

If my blue dress was going to Paris, I should really accompany it. And I should really have some more pieces on the catwalk as well. If *he* wasn't going to be there, then Paris could be a great opportunity for me.

"Quiet" by Jason Mraz played in the background. The song reminded me of Justin. Jason Mraz had always been our go-to musician. His voice could calm anybody, but it had a profound effect on us. We loved him. We loved each other when we were listening to him.

A nostalgic smile crested my lips. I'd been avoiding Jason's music—it hurt too much when Justin wasn't there—but for some reason, that night, I was compelled to listen to him.

Jason's voice lifted and rose over my workspace, calming the inner storm that had been raging for days. The world was a tumultuous, chaotic place, but Justin and I had always managed to find our peace in each other...until Blake died and Justin stopped letting me in.

I didn't know how much time to give him before making my next move. After enduring an encounter with *the man*, I knew I couldn't give up on my marriage. I loved my husband, and the Justin I fell in love with was still in there somewhere.

Throat clearing from the entrance made me look

up. I glanced across the wide-open space and my breath evaporated.

Justin.

His hair was disheveled, his tie askew. Dark bags shadowed his eyes, his pasty complexion a testament to how little he was sleeping. He peered up at the speakers attached to the corners of the ceiling, his skin paling even more. He almost looked ready to bolt from the room, but then his jaw set with determination. Scrubbing a hand over his evening stubble, he wove around the tables, checking out the large room as he went. He didn't speak until he was standing opposite me. The only thing dividing us was my large worktable.

"This place is bigger than I thought. Very...open."

My lips quivered as I smiled at him. "Yeah, it's... Echelon's all about collaboration, so..."

Justin nodded, his eyes skimming over the sewing mannequin behind me. The cobalt blue dress had gold leaves sewn into the sleeveless bodice. The skirt flared out at the hips and stopped just above the knee with a rippled gold trim. When the model twirled at the end of the runway, it would flare out like a party dress from the fifties.

His lips twitched with what I thought was a smile before he glanced at me. Our gazes touched for a brief moment, but he pulled away before a true connection could be made. Jiggling the case in his hands, he murmured, "I was going to go to the house, but thought I should swing by the office first."

He made his point without saying anything. Yes, he was not the only workaholic in our relationship.

"I'm just trying to catch up on some things." I placed the scissors down.

The song continued to wash over us. I stared at Justin until he looked up. As soon as I caught his eye, I held his gaze with everything I could, willing him to read my mind.

I love you. I'll hold your hand through anything. Please forgive me.

With a few rapid blinks, he dipped his head and placed his briefcase on the stool beside him. "I, uh..." He cleared his throat. "W-wanted to drop these off to you."

My face crinkled. Him stuttering in front of me was a brutal blow. I'd hoped it had been a one-time thing, but there it was again, a little "w-w" to slice my hope to shreds.

The buckles on his briefcase clicked, a sharp disruption to the gentle music. My heart started racing with foreboding as he pulled a large envelope from his case and handed it to me.

I curled my fingers and rested my hands on the table. "What is that?"

"Sarah, please just take it." His voice quaked.

With a wrinkled brow, I reached for the envelope.

"Inside are legal documents you need to sign. I've tagged the places."

"Legal documents?" My confusion came out loud and snappy. Ripping the envelope open, I peeked inside and skimmed the heading on the first page.

My nostrils flared and I threw the envelope at him like it'd burned me. "I'm not signing those."

"Sarah..."

"No!" My eyes flashed when I pointed at him. "I said 'til death do us part and I meant it."

"You also said you'd be faithful." He slapped the envelope down.

Crossing my arms, I backed away from it, my chin trembling as I tried to hold back the torrent of tears.

Divorce?

He was trying to divorce me?

I sucked in a ragged, tear-filled breath. The promise we'd made after Blake's funeral scuttled through my mind. Blinking at the impending tears, I stared at Justin's broken expression and said, "I'm sinking. I need you. *Please* don't let me go."

My words make him shrink. He knew exactly what I was talking about. That night. That promise.

His breaths were rapid and shallow as he punched out his resolve, pointing at the ground with each statement. "We've both been sinking for months. This isn't working. I'm just trying to be realistic."

"No, you're running scared."

"You cheated on me!" He threw his arms wide, his loud outburst slicing through the air.

"It was a mistake," I countered, in a voice so hoarse it could barely be heard above the music.

He scoffed and shook his head, throwing me a

dark look I'd never seen before. It was more bleak than angry, but it still hurt.

I fell onto the stool behind me. My insignificant voice barely had the power to fight back. "You said you were going to be there."

Guilt crested over his expression, but it was railroaded by a steely justification. His unflinching gaze told me all I needed to know. With a near lifeless voice, he pointed to the envelope and said, "You've got thirty days to file a response. It'll be easier if you do, but it'll proceed either way if you don't."

He snapped his briefcase shut then clipped out of the room before I could even form a rebuttal. The envelope sat on the fabric square, a yellow stain on what was meant to be a stunning black dress.

As if by some sick twist of irony, the song, the one from the night I'd been referring to, started playing the second he left me.

"Rough Water" had surrounded us the night of Blake's funeral. We'd lain in bed together, holding one another. Blake's sudden, horrific departure had made me feel like we'd been tossed into a hurricane. The only thing I had to keep me afloat was Justin. We'd clung to each other.

And he'd promised. *I'll never let you go.*

But he lied.

TWENTY-FOUR

JUSTIN

Slumping back in my seat, I kicked the edge of my desk and stared at the ceiling until the lights turned into fuzzy balls. Since serving Sarah with the divorce papers, I hadn't been able to think straight.

I rubbed my eyes with a snicker. "You haven't been thinking straight for a long time, you moron."

"Rough Water." I couldn't believe Sarah pulled that one on me. I still remembered that night with a chilling clarity. She'd been so distraught, letting out all her misery, while I lay there in tortured silence. When she begged me to hold her, I'd had no choice. Anything to wipe that broken look off her face. Her tears had soaked into my shirt, and all I'd been able to do was promise her that I'd never let her go.

When I'd uttered those words, I'd had no idea how hard moving on would be. No one told me how much of a hole Blake would leave behind. No one warned me just how incompetent I'd feel trying to study for a degree I didn't want while working a job I hated all in the name of making my parents proud. Meanwhile, I had to try to fake it at home, acting like my head was above water the whole time so I could keep her from sinking. I loved my wife, but I wasn't strong enough to be the husband she needed…and she proved that by sleeping with another man.

Part of me wanted to believe her drunken story. Her regret was obvious…and maybe enough for me to forgive her, but…

She ripped my heart out.

How could I hold her up again when I had nothing left to cling to?

"Justin," Clay snapped.

I jolted upright, straightening my tie and trying to act like I hadn't been slacking off.

The lawyer's eyes narrowed as he wandered in and dropped a file on my desk. "Got some new contracts I want you to proof for me."

Holding my sigh in check, I pulled them across my desk. "When do you need them by?"

"I have a seven a.m. conference call tomorrow." He hitched his shoulder, looking mildly rueful.

MELISSA PEARL

"Sorry for the late notice. I know you technically should be knocking off in five minutes, but I really need this done."

"Don't worry about it." I forced a closed-mouth smile. "That's what coffee's for, right?"

"It certainly is." He pointed at me. "Right, I better get home to the missus. Don't forget to give yours a call to let her know you're running late. I tell ya, that little trick has saved my marriage. Always let them know where you are and what time you'll be walking in the door. They'll forgive you anything if you just communicate with them."

I couldn't respond to his grin and wink. My mouth had flatlined and nothing was tugging that thing north.

Pressing my fingers into my forehead, I wondered if I could push hard enough to squeeze my brain out my ears. It felt slushy enough, maybe I could. I pushed at my forehead until my fingers started vibrating then gave up with a frustrated grunt.

Slapping my hands onto my desk, I forced myself to stand then shuffled to the break room. I hoped the coffee machine was still running. I'd take it as black and strong as I could get.

I was just about to turn down the corridor when a squeal from the front desk caught my attention.

With a wrinkled brow, I snuck down and peeked my head around the corner. Kelly was unwrapping a little cube-shaped gift on her desk. The smile taking over her face was stunning. I'd never seen her look so happy. Lifting the lid off the powder blue box, she tipped it up and caught the velvet case inside.

My gut twisted.

Her lips trembled as she popped it open then touched her chest.

"I made sure you can exchange it if you want." Marcus sounded nervous as he chuckled. He pressed his elbows onto the reception counter and leaned into view. I ducked my head back a little so he couldn't see me.

Her lips rose into a playful smile. "You did okay, Chapman." Pulling the ring free, she slid it onto her finger and held her hand out, swiveling it so the square-cut diamond could catch the light. The dreamy smile on her face reminded me of Sarah the day I proposed.

"Although…" Kelly raised her eyebrows. "Your proposal could do with some serious work. Come on, the office? Really?"

Marcus gave her a bemused grin. "Who said anything about me proposing? I bought you the ring." He shrugged. "I held up my end of the bargain."

She let out a horrified gasp then started laughing. "You're still expecting me to ask?"

He raised his eyebrows, his eyes dancing with mischief. "Well, you did mouth that Meghan Trainor song, and although you looked so damn hot doing that, I never actually heard you ask."

She slumped back in her seat, shaking her head at him. "You are so unromantic."

"Aw, come on, Kel, why should the girls get all

the romance? Don't you think that's just a little unfair? Why can't someone sweep me off my feet?"

"I will knock you off your feet if you're not careful." She pointed her manicured nail at him.

He snickered, licking his lower lip and sliding his hands into his pockets before sauntering around the desk. Taking a knee in front of her chair, he clasped her hands and gave her a smile that could melt any girl's heart. "I can be as romantic as you need me to be. All I care about is that you know how much I love you and that what we have is real. It doesn't need bells, whistles, roses, or sparkles—just you and me, Kel. That's it."

Kelly's lips drew into a quivering smile, her eyes glistening in the warmth of his gaze.

Marcus took a breath and grinned. "So, Kelly Rosina DeMarco…"

"Will you marry me?" she finished for him.

He jerked back with a surprised laugh. "You're asking me?" He pointed at his chest, looking like he'd just been handed the winning lottery ticket.

Kelly dropped off her chair, landing in front of him and wrapping her arms around his neck. "Yes, I am. Marcus, I love you more than I've ever loved anything. So, please, will you do me the honor of becoming my husband?"

"You know you've just made all my dreams come true, right?"

Her blushing smile was one for a wedding album. My fingers itched for a camera, wishing I could capture the moment for them.

Leaning back, Marcus gently took Kelly's face in

his hands. "There's nothing I want to do more than become Mr. Marcus Chapman. No, wait…" He tipped his head, pulling a playful expression while Kelly laughed. "To make you Mrs. Kelly Chapman."

Kelly pressed her forehead against his cheek while they laughed together. "You're an idiot."

He ran his hand up her back and squeezed the nape of her neck. "I'm your idiot."

She leaned back with a stunning smile, owning him with a soft murmur. "Forever and always."

I turned away the second their lips met. It was a beautiful proposal. So simple. So natural.

But it had nothing on mine.

Proposing to Sarah had been the most triumphant moment of my life. I'd spent weeks planning it—editing, splicing, creating a small piece of magic. Blake, of course, helped me set it up. He knew a guy who knew a guy. Everything fell into place so perfectly.

Sarah had no idea as we walked hand in hand to the movie theater that Blake and Jane were up in the booth. We settled in for the previews and my clip came up.

"I Love The Way You Love Me" started playing in time with images of Sarah. Some were stills, some were video footage of the two of us together. People in the audience started murmuring the second Sarah gasped. Her face was like the sun as she gaped at the screen. Three-quarters of the way through the clip, the footage changed to me as I held up individual signs—one for each word.

Sarah—Will—You—Marry—Me—?

She covered her mouth, frantically bobbing her head as she laughed and cried. She missed the last thirty seconds of the clip as she grabbed my face and kissed me.

The clip came to a wistful end, and someone from the front shouted out, "So, are you gonna say yes?"

Sarah lurched away from me and shouted, "Hell yes!"

The theater erupted with laughter and cheers. All eyes turned toward us as I awkwardly shuffled out of my seat and dropped to one knee so I could present her with the sapphire ring I'd had made from a design Jane copied out of Sarah's sketch pad.

Her sweet gasp filled my heart, her dreamy smile enough to fuel me for life. I slipped that ring on her finger and everything had been perfect.

TWENTY-FIVE

SARAH

The divorce papers sat in the middle of the dining room table. I'd dumped them there as soon as I got home from work on Wednesday, and I hadn't touched them since. I didn't know what I was going to do. I couldn't sign them. Honestly. I did *not* think I could physically do it.

I'd dated a couple of guys in high school, but it didn't take me long after meeting Justin to work out that he was the one. He surpassed any guy I'd ever even had a crush on. He was my soulmate, my best friend.

And I'd cheated on him.

Rubbing my stomach, I opened the fridge and stared at the contents. It was sparse—half a block of cheese, a rotting cucumber, two rubbery carrots, and the leftover Chinese takeout I'd ordered two nights ago.

Flicking the door closed again, I wrapped my arms around myself, curling my fingers into Justin's T-shirt and wondering how long the body could survive without food. I'd forced a bowl of granola into me each morning, but that was about it. I was out of milk, so I didn't know what the hell I was going to eat that morning. I didn't want to leave the house.

Having worked all day Saturday, I just needed a day at home to wallow.

But wallowing was hard work. I felt like I was wasting away. My energy was basically zip; I'd used it all up at work and talking to my mother on the phone Friday night. Thankfully, she'd spent most of her time going on about her romantic getaway with Daddy. I stomached every word and description. It meant I didn't have to talk about Justin and pretend my life was beautiful.

I managed to get out of the family dinner invite, using Paris as an excuse for me, and making up some big law assignment for Justin.

Mom was disappointed, but she understood, then told me to be careful I didn't work myself to the bone.

I promised her I wouldn't.

I lied.

Work was the only thing I had left.

How long could I keep the truth from her though? If I signed those divorce papers, I'd have to come clean to my family.

A shudder jolted my thinning body as I pictured the scenario. Dad's face, Mom's wide eyes.

Neither Justin nor Jane wanted to know who I'd *done it* with. But Mom, she'd go after those details. She'd want everything.

My throat felt full of marbles as I tried to swallow down the truth. It was awful.

Rubbing my neck, I swiveled for the kettle. Black coffee would have to keep me going until I could get to the grocery store. Blech. I hated it black, but with enough sugar...

The doorbell rang.

My heart spasmed and I nearly dropped the kettle. Smacking it onto the counter before I could spill water everywhere, I wiped my hands on my cotton pajama pants and shuffled to the door.

It was either Jane or my mother. I didn't want to see either, but my car was parked in the driveway, and both knew me well enough to know I wouldn't be out exercising.

"Shit," I muttered under my breath before yanking the door back. "Oh!"

A woman I'd never met before stood on my front steps. Her dress was designer—I recognized the cut immediately. Her dark locks were pulled into a stylish ponytail, and she was wearing a pair of chic shades. Perfect makeup, Prada handbag slung over her shoulder, and heels that cost more than my weekly wage. I knew exactly who the woman was. I'd seen photos on the wall at work.

She was carrying a paper bag with the words *Quirky Corner Cafe* printed on the side. The smells wafting from that thing made my stomach gurgle. Although I couldn't see her eyes, I could sense her calculating assessment of me.

A slow smile lifted her lips before she said, "Hi, I'm Kelly."

"I know who you are." My heart thundered. "What are...?" I licked my lips and gazed down at my bare toes. The chipped pink polish seemed so much worse in the light of a DeMarco. "What are you doing here?"

"I'm sorry to just show up like this. I thought if I called first, you might not let me come." The paper bag in her hand rustled as she held it up. "I was hoping I might be able to bribe you with a fresh blueberry muffin or some banana bread."

My traitorous stomach growled. Kelly snickered and gave me another once-over before raising her eyebrows hopefully.

But I didn't want the woman in my house. Why was she there? Did she know?

I blocked her way, trying to keep my voice smooth and easy. "How do you know where I live?"

Pulling off her shades, she gave me a kind smile. "I'm sorry if I overstepped my bounds, but I checked out Justin's file. His home address is listed, so..."

I rested my head against the door, remembering that Kelly worked at Torrence Records...on the same floor as Justin. "I'm guessing you know the ugly truth then."

"Uh…" Kelly glanced away from me then gave me a sheepish smile. "I've read between the lines." Her voice was even, neutral. "Justin hasn't said anything. I just saw some divorce papers on his desk and… well, I wanted to come and see how you were doing."

My forehead wrinkled. "Do you know why he wants a divorce?"

Kelly looked to the ground, pressing her lips together before finally admitting, "Justin wouldn't say, but…" She ran a finger over her right eyebrow. "Look, I know I shouldn't assume anything, but you're young and beautiful…" She paused before ending with a whispered, "And you work with my father."

A shuddering breath jolted out of me.

What was she saying? How would she know that working with her father would land me in this harrowing position? Did she think I was some swooning designer trying to sleep my way to the top?

I swallowed, a thick gulp that was actually audible.

Kelly DeMarco was standing on my doorstep, assuming I'd slept with her father…and she was right.

"It isn't what you think," I murmured. "I…" Shaking my head, I sniffed in a breath and raised my chin. "If you've come here with some kind of hate message, don't bother. I've said them all to the mirror already."

"I'm not here to do that." Kelly's gentle tone confused me.

"Um…why not?"

Her face twisted with agony. "Because I know my dad." Her expression hardened, the tormented sadness making room for a heated look of disgust. "He's…been doing this kind of thing for a while."

My belly knotted. *He has?*

"He likes a young, fresh face. I'm pretty sure he errs toward models, but you are one hot designer, so…" Kelly pursed her lips and looked over her shoulder, like maybe she was changing her mind about being here.

The tight ball in my stomach started bouncing, making me want to throw up again. I wasn't a one-off for Enrique; he'd done this kind of thing before. I couldn't decide if that made it better or worse. The man obviously slept around, no doubt when he was out of town. How long had he been doing it? How many young designers and models had he bedded?

I gripped the door, willing my legs not to give out.

Kelly, unaware of my inner panic attack, huffed then turned back to face me. "Thing is, you're the first one I've had access to, and it only took me one look to figure out that you're going through hell right now. I didn't know how I was going to react when you first opened that door. I had visions of smooshing blueberry muffin into your hair, but…" She smiled. "Now I just kind of want to talk to you.

And I promise I'll do my very best not to judge. I'm guessing you're feeling kind of lonely right now."

"How can you look at me like that? Like I'm not the scum of the earth?"

Her gaze softened, a small smile tugging at her glossy lips. "Because you just called yourself *the scum of the earth*. Trust me, I know what real remorse looks like. You're not faking it."

My eyes tingled with tears and I stepped back, making room for Kelly to enter. Her heels hit the wooden floor, sounding like sharp gunshots. I was a shrimp beside her. Motioning with my hand, I led her to the dining room table then stepped into the kitchen to grab two plates.

"Coffee?" I asked.

She nodded. "Sure."

"I've only got black…instant. Sorry, I'm kind of low on supplies right now."

"That's fine." I couldn't help noticing the sparkling ring on her finger as she unpacked the paper bag. Square-cut solitaire set in a white gold band. Looked pretty new. I gazed down at my sapphire, rubbing it lovingly as I waited for the kettle to boil.

We didn't say anything to each other as we set ourselves up to eat and drink. Kelly set out the plates, dividing the food between us while I made the coffee.

It wasn't until I slipped into my seat and started nibbling the corner of my muffin that she said anything.

"I'm really sorry." She wrapped her fingers

around the mug.

I gazed down at my plate and shrugged. "You shouldn't be the one apologizing. It was my fault."

"Was it?" Kelly sipped her coffee and set it back down. "My father, he..." She let out a disgusted huff. "I'm guessing he approached you that night, right?"

My shoulders slumped as I leaned my elbows on the table. "Justin was supposed to be there. He'd promised me he'd come, and when he didn't show, I was mad and then heartbroken." My voice wobbled. "Your father found me crying at the bar. He gave me a hug and then sat down and chatted with me about fashion and then menial things that didn't matter. He was trying to make me feel better, and I just wanted to forget about my failing marriage." I sniffed. "It's been falling apart since the honeymoon ended. We haven't even made it a year. It's just been hard work, and I don't know how to fix it. Since Justin's brother died, he just... He won't talk to me anymore."

I lifted my hands in a hopeless shrug. "I probably ended up blabbering that all to your father. I can't really remember. I was already drunk on shots when he ordered us a bottle of champagne. I felt like I couldn't say no. If anything, I was trying to hide the fact I was tipsy. I didn't want to embarrass myself in front of my boss." I rolled my eyes. "The show had gone so well, and he wanted to celebrate, and distract me. So I let him. I don't know when things turned fuzzy. I can vaguely remember my words starting to slur, and then I cried for a bit…and then he made me laugh." My expression crumpled.

Kelly's face bunched with sympathy. "He would have known what he was doing. My father's been cheating for years. My mom lets him get away with it. Their marriage is this sick, twisted beast that…" She shook her head. "It's not normal."

"Your mom knows?" I could barely whisper the words.

Kelly reached for my hand, giving it a quick squeeze. "I don't think she knows about you specifically. She just knows he's a cheater. Trust me, she's never going to do anything about it. The subject is completely taboo."

I buried my face in my hands and groaned.

"Hey." Kelly shook my wrist. "I'm not trying to make you feel worse. If anything, I'm blaming my father. Honestly, going after a distraught, drunk woman? That's a new low for him. He knew exactly what he was doing. Did he ask you to dance?"

With a loud sniff, I sat back and shook my head. "I don't remember all the details of the night. I definitely don't remember the trip up to his room. Things come to me in waves. Occasionally, I'll get hit with something that feels more like a dream than reality." My lips wobbled, my chin trembling as that sick feeling rose inside me again. "But I'll never be able to forget the horror of opening my eyes and finding the wrong man lying next to me." I felt like someone was poking needles into my eyes as I tried to deny the tears. My voice squeaked and croaked. "And then I realized what I'd done, and no matter how hard I wished for it, I couldn't take it back. I can't change it or undo it." Sobs shook my belly. "I want to turn back time. Why can't I do that?"

Tears rolled down my cheeks. I didn't bother to brush them away. Kelly stood from her seat and came around to my side of the table.

"Shh, it's okay." She rubbed my back in slow, soothing circles until my shuddering body calmed down to the hiccupy-breaths stage.

"Justin's miserable without you, you know. He looks like a lost stray. Those big, sad eyes."

I looked down at her. "I love those eyes."

"They are very kind," she whispered then smiled. "They're worth fighting for."

Standing up, she smoothed down her dress and pulled out the chair adjacent to me.

"Sarah, he's yours. Those eyes belong to you, and you need to convince him that he can't live without you. You're obviously sorry. And Justin's heart is big enough to forgive you, I know it is."

"He wants a divorce." I pointed at the envelope on the table. "It only happened two weeks ago, and he's already served me with the initial papers."

"He's still reacting out of pain. You cannot let him make a decision like this on impulse."

I sniffed, sitting back and staring at her with puffy eyes. "What am I supposed to do?"

Kelly's lips twitched then she leaned toward me. "I did a little snooping and found out he's staying at a motel just down the road from work. You need to go there and convince him to take you back. Slap some sense into him if you have to. Stop sitting here feeling sorry for yourself and do something about it. You want your husband back? Then go get him."

My lips parted, and I blinked at her a couple of times.

"Look, I know it's not really my place to get involved. Marcus told me not to come here today, but I just can't sit back and watch such a nice guy fall apart over this. I came here to see for myself what kind of person you are." She tapped my arm. "You know what, Sarah? I approve. I like you. I want to kill my father for putting you in this position, but more than that, I want to see you guys make it. Go on. Go win back your man."

TWENTY-SIX

JUSTIN

The rain was falling as I slumped home from work. By the time I reached my motel door, I was drenched through. For the record, briefcases make useless umbrellas. My shoes slapped against the ground then splashed into a puddle when I noticed Sarah cowering under the eaves. Her dress was sticking to her shapely body, her blonde hair dark against her pale cheeks.

She saw me coming and stood up straight, exposing herself to the slanting rain. I ran over to her and quickly opened the door, ushering her inside.

Dropping my case on the chair, I jumped around my overflowing sports bag and snatched a fresh towel from the bathroom. She hovered by the door, wiping the drips from her skin. Dammit, why'd she have to look so beautiful?

I threw the towel at her, too afraid to ask why she was there.

"I didn't see your car," I murmured.

She dried off her face and patted down her dress. "I parked around the block. I didn't want you to see it and not…come…"

My jaw worked to the side and I nodded, respecting her answer. Slipping the jacket from my shoulders, I threw it over the back of the rickety chair before ripping off my tie and unbuttoning my shirt.

Sarah's eyes roved my body when I exposed my chest to her. I met her gaze and she looked away. This was ridiculous. We were acting like we were about to have sex for the first time.

We weren't.

My eyes skimmed her dress, my body telling me something different.

I jerked away from the thought and strode to the stereo. The silence between us was suffocating. Music might ease the tension.

I let out a cynical laugh when I switched on the radio. "Without You" came on, forcing me to soften my bark to a hushed question. "What are you doing here, Sarah?"

"It's our wedding anniversary." She tucked the towel under her chin, her blue eyes filled with so much hope.

I knew what day it was. It'd been consuming me. In the life I thought we'd have, I would've been doing something really special. Wooing her all over again in some creative way.

But life hadn't turned out like we thought.

Dreams were easy.

Reality was impossible.

"What do you want from me?" I whispered.

"Forgiveness."

Her aching expression hurt. Pursing my lips, I tried to fight the sudden onset of tears. I wasn't crying. I hadn't cried since the day Blake died. I wasn't about to start now.

Man up, you wimp!

I swallowed and nodded. "Okay. And once you have that, then what?"

Sarah scraped a lock of wet hair off her cheek and hitched her right shoulder. "We move on. Forward. We keep going."

Dropping her towel, she gave me full view of her erect nipples. They were dark beneath the pale fabric of her wet dress. My groin stirred the more she inched toward me. I glanced to the floor, my chest heaving as I felt her approach.

"I don't know how it's going to work," she murmured. "I just know we have to do it together. We need to find our way back to each other."

The pads of her fingers landed on my shoulder, whistling over my skin as they traced down to my chest. She looked up at me, but I couldn't meet her gaze. My heart was thundering, my will to set her free fraying at the edges.

My hand worked of its own accord, drawn to her body by some magnetic force. Living without her had only fed my hunger. Having her standing before me in that sexy wet dress, her hair plastered to her glistening skin, my brain disintegrated, my animal instincts trampling common sense into the dirt. Trailing a path over her collarbone, I tucked my finger beneath the strap of her dress. Her nipples were still erect and I ached to touch them, to draw one into my mouth and remind myself of what it used to be like. My body yearned for sweet release.

Sarah's breath hitched, her eyes hopeful as she jumped all over my cue and slipped the dress off her shoulders, gliding it down her body. I watched it curve over her hips before dropping to the floor. Her slender legs stepped out of the wet mess, and she stood before me in nothing but her white, see-through underwear and shiny pink heels.

She looked thin, her skin stretched tight over her ribcage. I could make out each bone. My face buckled with concern, but my voice disappeared when she ran her soft touch up my chest until her arm was wrapped around my shoulders. She kissed my neck, and I felt myself fold. My arms snaked around her waist, slipping into the back of her panties and palming her tight little ass. She sighed against me, her tongue popping out to paint a line up to my earlobe. Her slender body pressed into mine, and the way her nipples pushed against the fabric of her bra had me standing to attention.

She must have felt it, because her butt cheeks tightened as she tipped her hips to rub against me.

"I love you, Justin," she whispered before sucking my lobe and grinding into me again.

She felt so damn good. I wanted to spin her around and lay her on the bed, spread her legs wide and then have them wrap around me as I buried myself inside her. I could see it all so clearly, the way she would bite her lower lip as she came, the feel of her fingers digging into my back... But before I could make a move, my brain decided to resurrect itself.

New images flashed before me. Unwelcome ones I couldn't counter. They threatened to tear me wide open. I squeezed my eyes against them, focusing on Sarah's tongue brushing my skin, the curve of her butt beneath my fingertips. I squeezed her to me and she moaned—that luscious sound that used to belong only to me.

Funny how one small sound can take a beautiful moment and rip it to shreds.

Her moan.

That was what did it.

I imagined that sound in another man's ear. Did she writhe beneath him? Did he make her come before entering her? How did he take her? Was she on her back or was he thrusting into her from behind? Snapshots flicked through my mind like some sick porno movie.

My head snapped back, my hands flying out of her pants.

"Justin?"

"I c-can't do this," I puffed, jerking away from her and landing on the bed behind us.

Sarah stared at me wide-eyed and sank onto the bed opposite me, wrapping her arms around herself. "You don't want me."

I let out brittle snicker. "It's not about want."

"It could be. You haven't touched me in months. I know I screwed everything up, but before Vegas…what did I do wrong? Why? Why didn't you want me anymore?"

"Is that why you cheated?" My eyes burned as I looked at her. "Because you think I didn't want you?"

"No! I cheated because I was drunk off my ass and I didn't know what I was doing!" She slapped the bed. "I never intended to hurt you! If you'd been there—"

"Oh, so it's *my* fault you let some guy shove his dick inside you?"

The room went still for a shocking beat, and then her face crumpled with a wounded sob. Covering her mouth, she curved over on herself and started to whimper like an injured kid.

Guilt slapped me in the face, but I couldn't apologize. I couldn't say anything. I'd never spoken to her like that before. It was mean, and I was a jackass for saying it. But all I could do was stare at her as she whimpered. Her shoulders trembled while she quietly cried in front of me.

Why couldn't I move to her? I wanted to comfort her, but my body just sat there—stupid and weak.

"I swear to you," she finally whispered, "I'll never do that again. If you could please just find it in your heart to move past this. I love you. I've only ever loved *you*."

"I can't touch you without thinking of—" *Blake's corpse…and now Mr. Vegas.*

"But…" she squeaked then sucked in a shaky breath. "I can't live without you."

Her broken whisper scraped down my spine, threatening to ruin me.

"Please," I croaked, "can you just go?"

She sat up straight, her blue eyes practically glowing. "I'm not leaving you, and I'm not signing those papers."

"You left me the second you cheated, don't you get that?"

"And you left me the day Blake died." She shot off the bed, standing over me in her skimpy underwear. I could see every muscle heaving as she begged me. "Please, I want you back. I *need* you."

"No, you don't." I shook my head. "You're better off without me, Sarah."

"Don't do this!" She slapped my shoulder then dug her nails in and gave me a firm shake. "Fight for me! Fight for us!"

Her desperate cries were met with silence. I couldn't respond. I didn't have any fight left in me. I'd been working myself to nothing trying to get over Blake's death…my guilt. How was I supposed to rise above her infidelity?

"Say Something" started playing in the background. It leaked into the room as a final warning. I kept my eyes on the carpet, gripping my curls like a failure.

The song washed over us—a melancholy refrain that threatened to drown me. I could feel Sarah's gaze on me as the words swirled around us. I glanced away from the carpet and spotted her thin fingers gripping the bed covers. The sapphire on her finger made my heart spasm. I squeezed my eyes shut and swallowed, my throat so viscous, talking was impossible.

Sarah finally let out a soft sigh and slipped back into her dress. I watched her shaky movements from the corner of my eye, resisting the urge to pull her into my lap and hold her against me.

She walked to the door and grabbed the handle, pausing to look back at me one last time. "Happy anniversary," she whispered. "For what it's worth, I'll never regret marrying you."

The door clicked shut behind her, and I was left with the mournful song and a shattered heart.

TWENTY-SEVEN

SARAH

I didn't realize I'd been waiting for the day to come, but I obviously had, because the second I woke up, it hit me like a battering ram to the chest.

It'd been one year since Blake's death.

Everyone would be feeling it, especially Jane…and Justin.

I'd sent him a text before leaving for work, but hadn't heard back. I could only imagine what torment was hounding him. He'd keep it all in though, locked away so no one could see it.

I worried my lip as I sat in the coffee shop below Echelon Fashion and waited.

The place wasn't busy. It was still summer, so most people were rushing in the door to get their fix then taking it outside. The sun was glorious, the sky so blue it looked like it went on forever. I gazed out the window, watching the light move and shift as people walked through its beams. Shadows danced on the pavement as two little girls skipped by hand in hand. They giggled and started to run when someone called for them to hurry. An elderly couple strolled past, nattering away like the best of friends. She had her wrinkled hand resting in the crook of his elbow. He looked down at her and said something that must have been sweet because she pressed her cheek against his shoulder while he patted her hand.

So cute.

So heart-wrenching.

I glanced back into the cafe, aware of traffic through the door. I hadn't seen Jane since she yelled at me, but I got a message on my phone while I was working. I dropped everything and left the office, telling Jules I'd pull an all-nighter if I had to. My friend needed me.

I hadn't realized how desperate I was to see her again. I'd kept my distance, giving her time to forgive me. Work was my salvation—the only thing keeping me afloat. I hadn't spoken to anyone outside of Echelon in days. Kelly had called to check on me, which was sweet. It was nice to have an ally. I couldn't believe how understanding she was over the whole thing. I didn't think I could be friends with a girl who screwed my father.

I shuddered, closing my eyes and thinking about those wretched divorce papers on my dining room table. I still hadn't signed them. Even though Justin wasn't willing to fight, I wasn't ready to let go. I wanted my husband back…I just didn't know how to reach him.

I'd left him a message the day after our anniversary, apologizing for yelling at him and asking if he'd be willing to do counseling with me…but I hadn't heard back. In retrospect, we should have had counseling after Blake's death, but everyone slipped into robot-mode and life passed by. We all thought we could be brave enough to do it on our own.

We were idiots.

The song on the radio switched to "Not Just You" by Ebony Day. I'd only heard it a couple of times before, but my soul seemed attuned to mournful music and I picked up on it right away. I closed my eyes and listened to the words, wondering if they were true.

I had hurt Justin, very badly.

But maybe he'd hurt me too.

I wanted to think that Vegas was a drunken mistake, but was there a part of me, buried deep in my subconscious, that allowed it to happen?

Was I somehow trying to wake my husband up? Pull him out of his stupor so that he'd see me again…let me in?

If that were the case, my subconscious needed a kick in the ass, because it was a complete and utter backfire. Slumping in my seat with a sigh, I gazed out the window. What a mess.

"I take it he hasn't forgiven you yet."

I whipped around at the sound of Jane's voice. She towered over me, her expression neutral. I held my breath and gazed into her green eyes. The yellow flecks in them were more obvious in the cafe light. With a soft sigh, my friend finally gave in and flashed me a brief smile. Slipping into the seat opposite me, she slid the bag off her shoulder and placed her elbows on the round table.

"Thanks for meeting me."

"Thanks for calling." I gave her a glum smile.

She picked at a groove in the table. "I just needed time."

"I know. I completely understand."

Tucking a lock of red hair behind her delicate ear, she studied me with narrowing eyes. "I didn't realize things were so bad for you two."

"I was drunk, Jane. I didn't..." I sighed, wondering if my *I didn't know what I was doing* line held up anymore.

"You wouldn't have been sitting in a bar doing that if you were happy. You're not a heavy drinker, you never have been."

"Never drink to make yourself feel better, right?" I muttered bitterly.

"You've never had to." She reached for my hand. "You've always been the sun, bright and glowing. Nothing could drag you down."

I placed mine on top of hers and squeezed. "Yeah, that's not actually true."

"All this time, I thought you were the invincible

one. I felt like a fool for feeling so depleted and lost without Blake. I tried to tell myself that you guys had each other, so it was easier for you." Her forehead crinkled. "But maybe it wasn't."

"It should have been. We should have held on to each other, but we just kind of drifted apart, both putting on brave faces and pretending like our marriage was…everything it needed to be." I sniffed. "I didn't mean to screw up so badly."

I swallowed, willing myself not to start crying again. I was so sick of tears.

"It was a mistake, Sparks. I understand that now, and I'm sorry for going off at you like I did. I was just horrified. It's so unlike you to do something like this. But after I had some time to reflect, I realized that you must have been feeling pretty damn desperate to put yourself in that position." Jane shook her head and looked out the window. "I just miss Blake so much, and I'm tired of feeling sad and empty all the time. Every day is an effort…and today, I mean, I don't even know how I would have gotten out of bed if Mom hadn't stood at my front door banging on it like a maniac."

I gazed down at my empty coffee mug, struggling to look at Jane's torn expression. So much pain.

"I can't keep going like this," she whispered. "It's been a year. Every day hauling my sad, tired ass out of bed and feeling numb. Going through the motions like a frickin' robot because if I let myself feel, I might just fall apart."

Her laughter was breathy and coated in tears.

"I'm not dying, Sarah. No matter how hard I pray for it, I still wake up every morning. I could live for another seventy-five years." Her eyes were desperate as she stared at me. "Seventy-five! I can't keep going like this. If I'm not going to die, then I need to figure out a way to live without him."

Her words crashed over me like a tidal wave, threatening to sweep me away. She'd been wanting to die? I pulled in a shuddering breath.

"So...what's your plan?" I asked.

Slashing at her tears, she scrambled in her bag and pulled out a rumpled piece of paper.

My forehead crinkled. "What's that?"

She smoothed it out on the table. "When we first moved to LA, I was miserable. I was the ginger kid with the weird name and a stupid accent. I missed England and I just wanted to go home. So, I ran away. I stole money out of Dad's wallet and I caught a bus to the airport." She rolled her eyes with a self-deprecating smile. "Of course, I forgot my passport and no one would sell me a ticket."

I snickered. "How have you never told me this story before?"

"I don't know." She shrugged. "Anyway, Mom came to get me. I blubbered out my misery and she hugged me and told me we'd come up with a solution together."

"And this is the result?"

I pointed at the sheet of paper. She flicked it across the table and I picked it up, scanning the bubbly writing.

Georjana's Bucket List

* *Disneyland*

"That's it?" I flipped the piece of paper over and gave her a bemused smile.

She wrinkled her nose. "About a week later, I made friends with another new girl at school, then I asked people to start calling me Jane, and before I knew it I was kind of loving my life. I didn't need it anymore."

"But you need it now."

"I don't know." She shrugged. "Is it a dumb idea?"

"It is if Disneyland's the only thing on here." Rummaging in my bag, I pulled out a pen and wrote beneath her original list.

Jane's Life List

"Okay, what do you want to do?"

She sighed and pulled a fresh sheet of paper from her bag. With a nervous half smile, she slid it across the table. Jane had already started a new list, and the first item on it was: *Say good-bye.*

"I'm going back to England, to the church. I need to start at the end, and find my new beginning."

I scanned down the rest of the list. It included random things, safe things, like: *eat at least one oyster, watch* Gone with the Wind, *read* The Great

Gatsby. Further down she started to get a little more adventurous: *Learn how to surf, try scuba diving, go skydiving, swim beneath a waterfall.*

My eyes shimmered with tears as I swallowed and fought the tingles in my nose.

"This is amazing."

"It's only a start. I just… I'm never going to fall in love again. Blake was the one, so I need to figure out life without him. I need to fill my life with things to keep me busy. To help me move on and forward. Maybe if I have a list to tick off, life on my own won't be quite so vacant."

"Are you sure going back to England's going to help you? Won't that be too painful?"

"I was in too much shock to really say good-bye. I'm hoping that going back will help me find closure. Blake and I had big plans for our honeymoon, so I'm going to go and do some of them." She tapped the list, indicating the skydiving and scuba diving.

Spinning my pen between my fingers, I added another thing to the list: *Horseback riding on the beach.* And then with a playful smile, I scribbled down: *Skinny dipping in the ocean.*

Jane gasped, but I just pointed at her and snickered. "You have to promise me."

A sound popped out of her mouth—one neither of us had heard in a really long time. It jolted both of us, and we stared at each other then both laughed. Laughed. Yes, Jane had actually laughed.

"That sounded really beautiful," I whispered.

Her lips wobbled into a crooked kind of smile.

"It felt pretty good too." Reaching across the table, she snatched my wrist. "This is crazy, right?"

"You better do it." My voice was low with conviction.

"I've already bought my ticket. I leave in a couple days. I only have a few weeks before school starts again."

"You can do a lot in a few weeks," I assured her. "You'll come back a whole new woman."

"Or maybe just a revised version of what I once was." Her smile was sad and wistful.

"You're making me realize that we've all been drifting this past year. Unless we do something about it, nothing's going to change. What I did…in Vegas was out of control. It altered everything, but not for the better."

"So, how are you going to make it better?"

I shrugged. "I need to take control. I need to stop waiting for everyone to start acting the way I want them to. We're not those two carefree girls from college anymore. Life's dealt its hand and knocked us on our asses. I've been desperately trying to live the life I thought I wanted, instead of accepting what is and carving out the life I actually need."

"I know exactly what you mean." She slapped her hand over her list. "Which is why I have to do this."

I smiled. "Do you want me to come with you?"

She paused to stare at me. "You'd do that?"

"I would if you needed me to."

"Well, I'd only accept if it fits with your plans."

She tipped her head. "What are your plans?"

Squeezing my eyes shut, I rubbed my forehead. "I'm still trying to work that out."

"What do you *need*, Sarah?"

I frowned, the weight of it all pushing me down in the chair. "I need the love of my life back. But I can't control that, can I?"

She shook her head. "I wish we could."

"So...what? Do I give him what he's asking for and then figure out what life looks like without him?"

Jane's expression was pained. "I guess that would be taking back control."

"I love him." My voice shook. "I love him so much."

"Do you think he still loves you?"

"I don't know. He's asking for a divorce, but I haven't been able to give it to him. How do I sign? It's the last thing I want to do."

"But maybe it's what he needs." Jane's eyes glassed over. "Maybe losing you will work like some kind of electric shock. He'll realize that he's making a big mistake."

"What if it doesn't?" My voice hitched with fear. "What if I never win him back?"

"Then you've got me, Sparks. Even when we're not together, you'll always be the best friend I've ever had, and I'm only ever one call away."

I grinned and hummed the first line of Charlie Puth's song, "One Call Away." She smiled and sang the second line, then we both sang the rest of the chorus together, Jane dropping into a perfect little harmony. It was a snippet of our past and one to treasure. We hadn't sung since the night before her wedding.

Every head in the cafe turned to look at us as we kept going with the song, singing at the top of our lungs like some sort of cathartic exercise.

It felt good to let go and just be me again. No pretenses, no show. I wasn't trying to hold anybody up or keep the threads together.

For the first time in a long time, I was just Sarah—the girl who thought life was beautiful.

TWENTY-EIGHT

JUSTIN

I had to move out of my motel. It'd been five weeks in that stuffy room, and I wasn't sure how much longer I could take it. Work was all-consuming. Everything else in my life sucked, and it was slowly killing me. Chipping away at the nothing I had left and turning me to vapor.

Sarah lingered in my mind constantly. I missed her. She'd always been the light at the end of my day, but I couldn't keep burning her out like I had. She gave her all to me and I'd given nothing back...so she'd found someone else's arms to hold her.

It didn't matter what I wanted. She didn't need my pathetic self in her life anymore. I was doing the right thing.

She only had a few days left to respond to the divorce papers, and then the long-winded process would begin. We wouldn't be officially divorced for months. I didn't want to think about it; I just had to take one step at a time and remind myself I was doing Sarah a favor.

Setting her free was the right move.

So why did it feel like a chain around my neck?

Slapping down the latest set of contracts, I shifted the file to my outbox only to find a new stack of folders beneath it. I scowled at the sticky note.

This is the last set for the week. I didn't want to overload you. I know you've got an assignment due Monday. Marcus has the reports you'll need to finish this.

Clay

I gave the note the finger, tempted to hurl the files off my desk. Pulling in a calming breath, I bunched my fists then sat down with clenched teeth. Flipping the folder open, I got to work.

Work.

Work.

Fucking work!

That was all my life consisted of, and I was miserable.

The clock ticked on the wall while I proofread

Clay's latest report. It was due by the end of the day. Rubbing my eyes, I tried to stop the letters blurring. I was so sick of legal jargon. The terminology blended into one big pile of gloop, and by the time I got to the end of the page, I realized I hadn't absorbed a word.

"Shit," I muttered, standing up and pushing away from my desk. I decided to pop in on Marcus and pick up those reports. I needed a break away from small black letters on white paper and computer screens.

Someone greeted me and I smiled, not really noticing who she was. Shuffling down the corridor, I turned toward Marcus's office. I knocked once and clicked open the door.

"Hey, man." He grinned at me.

He was pretty damn happy these days. Stupid engagement.

I gave him a tight smile. "R-reports for C-Clay?"

"On Kelly's desk, I think."

I nodded and went to leave.

"You doing okay?" Marcus called across the room.

People asked that question all the time, but when Marcus did, I knew he meant it…and I knew I couldn't answer. So I just walked away.

Neither Marcia nor Kelly was at the front desk. I didn't want to wait around, so I ducked into Kelly's workspace and started hunting. I didn't get far. My gaze was snagged by Kelly's computer screen.

"Sarah?" I whispered, recognizing my wife's email address. Ducking over Kelly's chair, I skimmed to the bottom of the messages so I could read the entire conversation between them.

Hey Kelly,

Just wanted to let you know that I'll courier those papers over this afternoon. Can you make sure Justin gets them okay? I'd like someone who cares about him to hand them over. Please look after him for me.

Thanks for everything.

xx
Sarah

*****

Sure. Of course, I will.
Are you doing okay? When do you leave for Paris?

*****

Tonight. The show's this weekend.

*****

Since when was she doing a show in Paris? I frowned and leaned a little closer to the screen, hating that I didn't know what she was up to. Yes, I was asking for a divorce, but I wasn't asking for the soul-crushing isolation that accompanied it. It made me realize how much I still wanted to be a part of her life. A show in Paris was a big deal. Pride soared through me before I even thought about it. I should have been there to hug her and celebrate with her. Instead, I'd been moping around my motel room, ignoring her texts.

Guilt wrinkled my forehead, and I berated myself for being such a selfish prick. She deserved to move on, to become a world-famous designer and be with someone who could treat her right. With a sharp huff, I went to move away from the screen, but my eyes skimmed Kelly's next message and I was pulled right back.

Good luck. I know you're scared.

Scared? Why? I scanned up the page, concern swamping me as I raced to read Sarah's reply.

Your dad's not going to be there. I don't think I could do this if he was. I've only spoken to him twice since Vegas. It's all been very professional, but I'd rather die than bump into him in a social setting again. I'm not going to touch a drop of alcohol while I'm away, but still…I just can't go there again.

My blood ran cold. I missed the rest of Sarah's response.

A penny fell through my brain, pinging off each circuit as a vile realization came to light. She'd never outright said it, but I wasn't stupid. There could only be one reason she'd want to avoid her boss in a social setting.

It'd been him.

Kelly's father. The head of Echelon Fashion. My wife had slept with *him.*

My stomach plummeted as I imagined his hands all over her. Having a picture made it a million times worse. The guy was old enough to be her father. What the hell had she been thinking? It was sick.

And she was still working for him.

She'd signed our divorce papers and was flitting off to Paris. Everything I wanted, right? For Sarah to be happy and successful...for her to move on. But not with a married man. What kind of asshole does that? Not only did he cheat on his wife, he went after mine as well!

I stumbled away from the chair, breaths punching out of me as I gripped the back of my neck.

Kelly appeared around the corner with a coffee mug in her hand. "Oh, hi. Can I help you with something?"

She took a sip and set the mug down while I backed out of her workspace and splayed my hands across the reception counter.

"You knew," I seethed. My voice was a low, gravelly murmur.

She looked up with a confused frown. "Excuse me?"

"You fucking knew!" I slapped the shiny veneer, making her jump. I didn't care; I was too riled to think straight. "You rich, pretentious assholes think you can have whatever the hell you want. Does your father not have enough? Huh? He had to take the one thing most precious to me?" I roared across the counter.

Kelly's skin paled, her eyes darting to her computer screen before closing with a sick look of guilt.

"Oh, yeah, that's right. You think I'm stupid. Trying to hide this shit from me. Geez, Kelly! You—"

My words were cut short by a rough yank to my jacket. Marcus spun me around, grabbing my collar and slamming me back against the desk. His thunderous look could have melted iron. "Don't you dare speak to her that way."

I wrestled his hands off me and shoved him back. "She knew. She knew this whole time!"

"And you didn't want to!" he yelled back. "You haven't wanted to talk about this once, so don't be yelling at her." Marcus pointed at a wide-eyed Kelly. "You need to take a good look in the mirror, my friend, and stop blaming everyone else around you for your own misery."

Heads had poked out of offices, checking out the drama. I felt each and every gaze, my cheeks spiking with color as I shakily tugged my jacket down.

Spinning on my heel, I stormed for the exit, shoving the door open with my shoulder and racing down the stairs. I didn't want to look in any damn mirror. I wanted to find the nearest bar and forget life existed.

TWENTY-NINE

SARAH

"Distance" played throughout the house as I folded my clothes and got ready for Jules to collect me. As far as I knew, it was just the two of us going for the Paris show, plus Michael was joining us from the New York office. Echelon wasn't hosting the event like they had in Vegas. We were being featured as part of a collaborative venture between several fashion houses, which was why Enrique probably didn't feel the need to attend. If he wasn't front and center, he wasn't interested.

I scoffed out a bitter laugh.

Why was I still working for him?

Because I needed the money. The opportunities at Echelon Fashion were too big. I was on my way to making a name for myself. How could I just walk away from that? I no longer had a marriage, so I had to make the most of my career.

It was something I could control.

Whether or not it was the right decision, I wasn't sure. All I knew was that Paris would be a good break away from everything in LA.

The doorbell jerked me out of my stupor.

I headed down the stairs, snatching the divorce papers off the edge of the dining room table before answering.

The courier stood there with her scanner.

"How's it going?" she murmured, not really caring what my answer was.

Checking the address and the label, she scanned the sticker then tucked my life beneath her arm.

"It'll be there by five."

"Thank you," I whispered, watching her trot down the stairs and into her van. She gave me a quick wave before reversing out of the driveway. I closed the door and leaned against it, my hair going up as I slid down.

My butt hit the floor and my arms flopped down.

There it went.

My marriage.

I turned in slow motion to stare at the stereo, the melancholy words washing over me as I whispered, "I love you, Justin."

THIRTY

JUSTIN

The bar was a lonely place at four o'clock in the afternoon. It was a seedy little joint down the road from Torrence Records. I'd eaten there a couple times on the way home from work. The night crowd was rowdy and distracting.

The afternoon crowd...not so much.

Some country tune was whining out of the jukebox. I didn't know it, but it was talking about drinking beer and life being sideways, so it suited me just fine.

A couple of older guys with round guts played pool in the back corner. One of them was sporting an impressive beard that reached nearly to his collarbone, while the other had a chin dimple that looked like it'd been made with an axe blade.

A baseball game was playing on the television, and the barman was as far away from my miserable ass as he could get. My vision was slightly blurry as I pressed the beer bottle to my lips and took a sip. I wasn't that drunk—too much proofreading was turning my eyes to fuzz.

I had to get out of my damn job, but where the hell would that leave me?

Jobless.

Homeless.

Wifeless.

I was pathetic.

The bar door swung open and Marcus walked in. I groaned and turned away from him, swiveling so my body was angled at the pool tables.

He sat down with a snicker, slapping me on the shoulder before ordering himself a beer.

"So, this place is nice."

I rolled my eyes and glared at him.

"It must be making you feel a whole lot better." He looked around, his eyebrows rising. "I don't see any mirrors though."

"W-would you shut up about the d-damn m-mirror."

"I'm not trying to be a condescending prick, okay? I just want to help you." He sighed. "You've been miserable for weeks and you're not doing anything to change that."

"What am I supposed to do?" I snapped.

"Figure out what makes you happy and go after it."

"I-I can't have what makes me h-happy," I growled. "S-she deserves better. I've looked in the fucking m-mirror and all I see is a d-damn failure. A guy who hates his life." I slapped the bar. "She's the s-sun, man. She's so beautiful and I...I can't even love her." I shook my head, my eyes burning with tears.

Marcus studied my face with a sad smile. "But you *do* love her."

"I can't be enough," I croaked. "She cheated on me, b-because I wasn't enough."

"That is such bullshit." Marcus accentuated the T. "Do you honestly think if she wanted more than you, she would have refused to sign those papers?"

"She did sign them! They're being couriered over as we s-speak."

"Yeah, after nearly a month of contention. She did *not* want to sign those papers."

"Then why did she?" My voice was small and wobbly as I cradled the beer bottle against my chest.

Marcus gave me an incredulous look and bulged his eyes at me. "Because you've left her with no other choice."

I grunted then drained the bottle. Slapping it on the counter, I indicated to the barman that I'd like another.

Marcus shook his head. "No, he doesn't."

My glare was dark, narrowing my eyes to fine slits.

Marcus tutted and shook his head. "So, that's it. You're just gonna roll over and take it? Turn yourself into a bitter old bastard, because your wife cheated on you, one time…and she told you about it the second she got home…and she begged you to forgive her."

My eyebrows dipped so low my forehead started to hurt.

"You know, it sounds to me like *you're* the one who's looking for the easy out."

"That is not true!" I shot off the stool, leaning over him and pointing in his face. "I love her. I have loved her since the day I saw her!"

"Then why are you in this shithole getting drunk? Shouldn't you be hauling ass over to your place right now? Winning her back?"

My chest deflated as I thumped back onto my stool. "I-I don't know how to move past this a-agony inside me. How do I-I love her the way she d-deserves? I don't even f-feel like a complete p-person anymore."

Marcus gave me a compassionate smile before squeezing my shoulder. I'd told him about Blake months ago, brushed over the shocking details then told him I didn't want to talk about it, ever again.

"Tell me this… Does having Sarah in your life make the agony worse?"

"Of course not." I tipped my floppy head. "I'm miserable without her."

"Then make a choice, man. Choose right here, right now, to forgive her. Choose to be the man she deserves. *Choose* to love her for the rest of your life.

You may not do it perfectly, but love doesn't have to be perfect. It just has to be real."

I gazed at him with glassy eyes. His words landed on me and were sucked right into my chest.

"I'm not saying it's going to be a walk in the park. Life's dealt you guys some vicious blows, but the only thing that's going to make you a failure is if you don't try to overcome them. What kind of ending are you looking for, man? 'Cause right now, you're starring in your own tragedy. But there's no law saying you have to stay in it."

The music changed. It was like this weird moment where Marcus's words and the new music created this supernatural kind of lightbulb experience.

I snapped my head around to gaze at the jukebox.

Mika was singing.

His voice had drawn my eyes to Sarah in the first place, and it was his song that was lashing me now. My mouth dropped open as "Happy Ending" played throughout the bar. Would his voice lead me back to her?

Having spent the last hour listening to country music, the song stuck out like a throbbing red thumb. Did I seriously want to spend the rest of my life without her?

"Little bit of love," I whispered.

"That's what I'm saying, man. It's up to you. Let go of this horseshit that you're not good enough and embrace the fact that she chose you in the first place."

My nostrils flared, my heart jolting like it'd been hit with a defibrillator. Lurching off the stool, I ran for the door, my mind screaming as I dashed back to the office to grab my stuff. Marcus was right. Sarah had chosen me...just like I'd chosen her. Yeah, we hadn't hit any roadblocks at that stage, but we'd made a commitment. I'd made a promise to love her, and now I had to make a choice to keep on doing that in spite of her betrayal, and in spite of my nothing center. I had to rise above all that shit. I had to start acting like the man I thought Sarah deserved.

Fear skittered through me as I bolted back to Torrence Records. Could I do it? Could I be that man?

"Yes," I growled. "You fucking can."

THIRTY-ONE

SARAH

I followed Jules down the narrow aisle and waited for him to stow his luggage before passing him my bag. He slotted it into place then stepped aside so I could have the window seat.

"Thanks." I sat down and buckled my seatbelt.

My hands were still shaky. They had been since I signed those divorce papers.

I couldn't believe it was over.

Resting my chin on my knuckles, I gazed out the little plane window. We were sitting just behind the wing. It was the same view I'd had on the way to England. Justin's hand had been on my knee as we prepared to travel overseas for the first time. I'd traveled a little, but we'd never gone anywhere together, and certainly not as husband and wife.

I'd threaded my fingers through his and smiled down at my gold ring. It sat perfectly beneath my glistening sapphire with the diamonds either side. He said as soon as Jane had shown him the design from my sketchbook, he knew he had to make it happen for me.

Blake told me later that Justin had borrowed money from his parents to have the ring specially made. I'd always loved sapphires. The stone reminded me of clear blue skies and crystal waters.

Justin said the color made him think of my eyes, and that's why he loved the ring so much.

I glanced at my fingers, adjusting my engagement and wedding rings so they sat straight. They'd lost their sparkle, much like my eyes had. I needed to get the rings cleaned, but…

"You okay, *chica*?" Jules nudged me with his elbow.

"Yeah." I nodded. "I'm gonna be fine." I was determined to make that statement true. Jane would leave for England the day I landed in Paris. She'd done some whirlwind arranging and was off to discover herself. It made me sad to think she had to. It made me even sadder to think that I did too.

I didn't know how I was going to do it.

But at least Justin was getting what he wanted. That gave me a small sense of peace.

Julian's phone dinged. He pulled it free and read the text, his mouth lifting with a grin.

"Your boyfriend?" I couldn't help asking.

"No." Jules shook his head with a grin. "The boss."

My stomach hitched.

"He's decided to swing by Paris after Rome. He'll make it for the show after all."

"Oh, great." I couldn't have sounded enthusiastic if I'd wanted to. My voice was flat and dead. I didn't want to see Enrique in Paris. I didn't want to have to party with him after the show and put on a brave smile, pretending like what we'd done in Vegas was something we could just forget about.

I didn't know if I could ever forget, and then having to face the cause of my demise outside of work... I'd promised myself I'd tell my family when I got back from Paris.

Threading my fingers together, I squeezed hard in an attempt to quell the shaking.

What the hell was I going to do? Life would never be the same for me again.

THIRTY-TWO

JUSTIN

I sprinted past reception and up to my desk. I had no idea what time Sarah's flight left. Did I really have the right to stop her? It was a big deal, going to Paris, and I didn't want to do anything to hinder her career.

By the time I reached the exec floor, my brain had slowed enough to figure out that it'd be best to wait until Sarah returned before making my big move.

But I was going to make it.

I was sure of that.

I'd move back home while she was away, and

when she returned, I'd be there with an open heart and nothing but raw honesty.

If I had to cry in front of her, then so be it. If that was what she needed from me, then that was what I'd give her. I'd never wanted to pour my emotions out so badly in my life. I'd always been about keeping it in, locked down...and where had that gotten me?

I sped down to my office, bustling past people who were packing up for the day. They'd be heading home at any minute, leaving work to go and hang out with their loved ones.

That was going to be me again.

Sarah deserved to have someone love her. Not some rich asshole who was already married, but me. The guy who would have done anything to make her happy. I might have failed as a son, as a law student...even as a brother. But I wasn't going to fail Sarah. I could love her better than anybody.

We *would* get that happy ending. It wouldn't necessarily be perfect, but it'd be ours.

Swerving into my office, I jerked to a stop when I noticed a new pile of files on my desk. A bright orange sticky note curled up from the center of the top file.

For Justin. Need these by Monday morning.

Everett's name was slashed across the bottom.

I picked up the stack with a dark scowl and huffed out a breath, my upper lip curling.

"Screw this," I muttered, and with a roar

slammed them into the trash can before storming out of my office.

I took the stairs up to Everett's floor. Walking straight past his receptionist, I pounded on his door once before barging in.

"Everett, we need to talk." I flicked my jacket back and rested my hands on my hips.

"Sorry, sir." His secretary scuttled in behind me. "He just walked right past me."

"That's okay, Annie. I'll take it from here. You get ready to head on home."

"Okay. Thank you, sir. Have a good night."

"You too." He smiled before turning his gaze to me. The cordial expression slipped from his face the second she was gone. "You better have a damn good reason for barging into my office this way. You're lucky I wasn't on a conference call."

"My reasons are good, believe me." I blinked, suddenly aware that I hadn't stuttered once since stepping into the room. Sucking in a breath, I puffed out my chest and kept going. "Everett, I have to quit this job. I hate it. I always have."

Rising from his chair like a giant sea monster, Everett slowly buttoned his jacket and pierced me with a look I was so used to shrinking away from. "Then why the hell did you take it?"

I stood my ground. "B-Because, I wanted to make her happy. I-I thought if I c-could just work hard enough, then everything would be okay." I swallowed, willing my strength not to fail me. "It's not okay." My eyes started stinging. "I need to make it right, and part of doing that is quitting this

MELISSA PEARL

job. I can no longer give a shit if you don't think I'm good enough for your daughter. I have spent my life trying to excel in every area I thought mattered, yet I failed at the most important one."

My voice trembled, but my stuttering was under control, so I kept going, grinding out the words with everything I had.

"Sarah cheated on me."

Everett balked, his brows dipping into a thunderous frown. "How dare you talk about my daughter that way."

"It's the truth. So, I asked her for a divorce, and she's finally giving me one. She signed the papers today. And you know what? I've never felt worse in my entire life." Emotion got the better of me. The stinging in my eyes turned to water as I stared down the man I'd spent so many years trying to impress. "I promised her that no matter what we had to go through, I would never give up on us. I'd never let her go…and what did I do? The first sign of trouble and I let her fall right through my fingers." My hands shook as I held them up—two empty palms. "I'm tired of feeling this way. I'm not letting go again."

My voice rose as the tears I'd been denying myself since Blake's funeral finally trickled free. "I can't manage this life without her, and if I'm going to give her my best, I've got to get out of this place. I quit. And I'm quitting law too. It's time for me to stop trying to impress everyone else. The only thing that matters is getting Sarah back. Think whatever the hell you like, but for the first time in

222

my life I'm fighting for something that actually matters."

Everett had no response. He just stared at me in stunned silence while I slashed the tears off my face and walked out of his office. The second I reached the elevator, I drew in a deep breath. My chest actually expanded all the way, like it was finally capable of taking in the oxygen I needed.

Traveling down a floor, I found my lips curling at the corners as I relived the look on my father-in-law's face. I couldn't believe I'd actually gone off on him like that. It'd felt amazing. My mind then flicked to Sarah, and my smile grew to full beam. When she walked in the door after Paris, I'd be waiting there with open arms...open everything. I didn't care how long we had to talk; we were working our shit out.

We needed a fresh start—a new home, definitely a new job for me.

If she wanted to keep working for DeMarco, then that was up to her. It'd be something I'd have to come to terms with. Something we could *talk* through together.

Talk through together.

Damn that sounded good. Slightly terrifying, but really good.

I paused at Kelly's desk, ready to apologize for acting like a madman earlier, but she wasn't there. I'd look for her before I left. With lighter feet, I headed down to clear my desk. I was leaving Clay and Everett in the lurch, but I was positive a few hundred applicants would be just around the corner. It was a lush job with a good company. Someone who was actually passionate about contractual law would love it.

Striding into my office, I looked up to find Kelly placing an envelope on my desk. She must have heard me coming because her sad frown was already in place.

"These are for you," she murmured then looked up at me with hopeful eyes. "Do you still want them?"

I just smiled at her.

"Oh, thank God." She tipped her head back, touching her chest with relief. "Okay, you've gotta go."

"What?"

She spun her hand with an urgent gesture. "I'll drive you to the airport myself."

"What are you talking about?"

"Hello!" Her eyes popped wide.

I raised my hand to calm her down. "No, it's okay. I'm not stopping her success in Paris. When she gets back, I'll be waiting at home for her."

"No, that's not good enough." Kelly's dark hair swished as she shook her head at me.

"Kelly, I've just quit my job. I can't afford to fly to Paris."

Her shocked surprise was quickly bulldozed by another expression that had a ripple of fear curling in my belly. Her eyes glittered with a mixture of guilt and shame.

"What?"

"You can't wait until she gets back."

"Why not? It'll give me a chance to get out of here, move back home, think of what I'm going to say to her…" My voice trailed off as Kelly's eyes began to glitter. "What?" I snapped.

She spun the engagement ring around her finger, struggling to make eye contact. Her gaze kept flicking over mine then back to the files in the trash can. "I just found out that my dad's going to be in Paris after all."

Her words slapped me in the face. I blinked then swallowed, my nostrils flaring as I grappled to hold on to my composure. "Doesn't matter. She won't do it again. I trust her."

"It's not about trust. She didn't mean to cheat on you the first time. My father…" Kelly huffed, making two fists before dropping her hands to her sides. Her voice was small and filled with shame. "He's an asshole, okay? He totally seduced her. She was downing shots when he found her. She can't remember much, but she said he bought them a bottle of champagne. He totally took advantage of her, Justin."

"What!" I spat. "Are you saying he—?"

"I'm not saying he violated her." Kelly held up her hand then gave me a pained frown. "I'd like to think my father has just a touch more class than that, but…" She sighed. "Look, when Sarah says she can't really remember, she probably can't. I'm guessing she was off-her-ass drunk and got caught up in a moment. My father should have walked her to her room and put her to bed, but instead he…"

A new kind of rage I'd never felt before bubbled

inside me. It was a struggle to talk as I pictured my wife's floopy body being guided to *his* hotel room. She giggled a lot when she was tipsy, and she got really affectionate. Was that what she had been doing with him? Was that why he thought he had the right to strip her naked and have sex with her?

"Do you think he'll do it again?" My voice had an edge so sharp it almost vibrated.

"Look, I don't know. I just… He saves his affairs for traveling. He likes to put on the show that he's the perfect husband, so his little trysts are always out of town. He travels a lot, so…" Kelly pushed her finger into the corner of her eye and started blinking like she was fighting tears. "I just hate the idea of Sarah being vulnerable again. She's just signed these divorce papers. She didn't want to. She's not in a great place…" Kelly released a shaky sigh. "I do think you're right to trust her, but my father…I'm not so sure."

"I should've been there to protect her," I croaked.

Kelly's eyes locked onto mine. They were bright and fierce, perfectly matching the tone of her voice. "Do you want to make that same mistake twice?"

I scrubbed a hand down my face, images of Sarah's sweet smile flashing through my brain. Tipping my head out the door, I turned on my heel and growled, "Let's go."

THIRTY-THREE

SARAH

I was shattered. The eleven-hour flight had been bearable, but keeping up a happy façade for Jules was exhausting. He prattled on about his love life for most of the trip, while I pretended to be the happily married wife who wasn't freaking out that her boss was going to make another pass at her in Paris.

"I should have just quit after Vegas," I muttered to myself, flipping open my suitcase and digging out my toiletries.

We'd gone straight from the airport to the venue, spending a few hours there unpacking our designs and checking everything was perfect for the show the next day. After that, Jules forced me to a fancy restaurant where we ate French food and he tried to get me drinking French wine. In the end, I had one glass just to shut him up. The food had been delicious…and I couldn't enjoy a single bite.

My stomach was a mass of knots.

All I wanted was a hot shower and sleep. If I looked the way I felt, I wouldn't even be allowed access to the show. It'd be a huge day prepping all the models, making sure each outfit sat perfectly on them. Enrique wanted ours to look the best, of course, so Jules, Michael, and I would be under huge pressure. Some bigwigs in the fashion industry would be there. That's why Enrique changed his mind about coming—the guest list had improved.

With a shuddering sigh, I slipped off my clothes and headed for the shower. I hoped Jane had an easier time finding her way. Because I felt completely lost.

Maybe I should be joining her after Paris?

A knock at the door made me flinch. Heaving a sigh, I pulled on a hotel bathrobe and wound it tight around my waist before checking the peephole.

Enrique's face was warped through the fishbowl glass, his nose elongated as he leaned in close.

"Shit," I muttered. Alone in a hotel room in nothing but a bathrobe, with that guy outside my door. I'd never felt more vulnerable. I pressed my head against the wood and prayed he'd go away.

"Sarah, I can hear you behind the door. Please open for me." His Italian accent, so smooth and sexy, sent a cold shudder down my spine.

Gripping the handle, I squeezed my eyes shut and held my breath.

Enrique cleared his throat and knocked again. "I'm not leaving until you let me talk to you."

I sucked in a breath and pulled the door ajar, just wide enough for him to see my face. "No."

Enrique wasn't even put off by my icy greeting. If anything, it made him smile. "I have bought you champagne, my dear. We are in Paris. It is a time of celebration."

"I have nothing to celebrate with you."

"You are one of the youngest designers represented at this show. Talent like yours should always be celebrated. Tomorrow will be spectacular. I can't wait to show you off once more." His voice dropped to a husky whisper as he brushed a champagne flute gently down my cheek.

I flinched away from the glass. "You need to go."

"Oh come, *cherie*." He winked, obviously thinking his French endearment was oh-so charming. "We had such a wonderful time together in Las Vegas."

With a scoffing laugh, I shook my head. "You had a good time. I ruined my life."

He pulled a face that told me he was trying to brush off my insult.

"Is that why you came to Paris? So we could be together again? Screw me while we're out of town and your wife can't find out?"

He ignored my jabs, acting like I'd just told him he was sexy. His eyes wrinkled at the corners. "I could be with one of a hundred models right now, but I'm choosing you. You enchant me, Sarah. I can see wonderful things in your future. So much potential. Let me guide your way."

"How is sleeping with me guiding my way?"

His roguish grin would have been charming if I weren't so disgusted by it.

"I want you to leave." I hated how much my voice shook.

"*Bella*, I can make your career. We could do wonderful things together."

Gripping the door, I blinked a couple of times then let out a revealing snicker. "All I ever wanted to do was design clothes that would make people feel beautiful. I thought working for you would be the best job in the world, that I would be the happiest version of myself while I stood in your amazing building and created to my heart's content."

He nodded, but his gaze was drifting down my body, no doubt working out that there was nothing but a bathrobe between him and my skin.

"But you know what I've worked out? I can't create to my full potential working for you. You stole my heart's content that night you took me into your bed. Shame on you. I was a married woman. I should have never let you touch me." I ended with a dark whisper. "I quit."

His eyes shot back to mine. "You can't quit. You

are going to be my star protégé."

"No, I'm not." I sniffed, biting my lips together and shaking my head. "It's all worthless without him. Please, just leave."

Standing his ground, he studied me with a look that would probably make most girls swoon. I didn't know what else to say to him, and I didn't have the energy to stand and fight anymore.

"You can't do this, Sarah. I will not let you quit. You're too talented."

"Just leave," I whimpered.

When he opened his mouth to yet again rebuke my resignation, I closed my eyes and rested my head on the door. If he said one more word, I was going to slam it in his face. He'd no doubt stand there knocking until I let him back in.

Tears burned as desperation tried to blind me.

But then a firm voice in the hallway saved my life. "She asked you to leave."

I'd never heard such a steely tone coming from him before. I almost didn't recognize his voice, but my heart knew…and damn, if it wasn't the sexiest thing I'd ever heard.

Peeking my head out the door with a gasp, I spotted Justin a few feet away. His dark glare was aimed straight at Enrique.

The tall Italian smirked, his long, chiseled face oozing contempt. "And who are you?"

Justin pulled his shoulders back, his chest puffing out just a little as he growled, "I'm her husband."

My heart grew wings and fluttered around my

ribcage. Enrique took a quick step away from me before giving Justin a charming smile. "Welcome to Paris. Sarah and I were just discussing details for the show to—"

"Don't." Justin cut him off. "I know exactly what you were doing."

Justin wasn't stuttering. He was breathing like a bull ready to charge. I'd never seen him so angry before. Waves of rage pulsed out of him, pushing the tall Italian away.

Enrique swallowed, lifting his chin and holding out the champagne bottle and glasses. "I'm sure I don't know what you mean; however, I will leave you two to enjoy your evening. *Ciao.*" As soon as Justin took the bottle and flutes, Enrique strode away as if he'd just performed an act of charity.

Justin cursed under his breath and slipped into my room, placing the bottle and glasses down before spinning to face me.

"I'm allowed to hate that guy, right?"

"As much as you like. He's not my boss anymore." I tittered, a nervous, edgy sound that gave away the force of the emotions zinging inside me.

Justin stilled, his expression softening as he drank me in. "You really quit?"

"You really still my husband?"

The side of his mouth tipped up with a smile. He slipped the bag off his shoulder, letting it gently thump to the ground beside him. I gazed at his sports bag, the one he'd stuffed full of clothes the day he left me. It looked haphazardly packed once more, with funny bulges out the side. The white airline tag sagged toward the floor.

He'd flown all the way to Paris.

For me?

Hope set my heart beating out of time. I didn't know what to say to him. Did he want me to run into his embrace? Stand there and listen? What?

I drew in a shaky breath and crossed my arms, gripping the bathrobe material in my fist.

Justin ran a hand over his curls and gazed across the room at me.

"Thing is, Sparks, I made you a promise." His eyes started to glisten as his voice dropped to a husky whisper. "I said I'd never let you go."

The storm of emotions that had been living inside me for months zipped out of my mouth in a gasping sob. I covered my lips to try to contain it, but it didn't work. The sound shot across the room, tugging Justin toward me.

"C'mere," he whispered against my cheek, lifting me off the ground and carrying me over to the bed. I curled my arms around his neck as he sat us on the edge and held me close. Running his arm up my back, he squeezed the nape of my neck and murmured into my ear. "I'm sorry for taking so long. But I'm here now, and I'm not leaving you again."

His soft words swirled through me—replenishing, refilling, rejuvenating everything that had withered.

I sat up and wriggled around on his lap until my knees were on either side of him. Running my hand down his cheek, I drank in his beautiful face. "You sure?"

He brushed my tears away with his thumbs, and then did something he hadn't done in a really long time...

He initiated a kiss—something so small and insignificant, yet so incredibly huge.

His full lips brought me back home, reminding me of everything we'd had before and everything that could be washed away if only we'd let it.

I leaned into the kiss, pressing my body against his strong torso and silently pleading for more. His tongue circled mine and we fell back in step, creating a familiar dance we'd performed hundreds of times in the past. Our bodies still remembered all the moves.

Slipping the bathrobe off my shoulders, I wrestled out of the fabric, wanting to present him with everything. His hands brushed my bare shoulders before he pulled away from me. With a nervous swallow, he scanned my body, his eyes flashing with desire as he studied my naked torso.

"What if I hurt you?" he whispered.

I jerked away from him. "What are you talking about?"

"Last time..." His face bunched with anguish. "I hurt you, I..."

My lips parted as my eyebrows slowly rose. "Is that why you haven't touched me? I thought you didn't want me."

He closed his eyes and cringed before cupping my breasts and gently kneading them. "How could

I not want you? You're the most beautiful person on this planet."

My nipples reacted to his touch, sending tingles of pleasure racing through my body. I couldn't help a soft sigh as I dipped my head so our cheeks pressed together. "You never hurt me."

"I did." He moved away so he could look me in the eye. "I know I did."

"It felt good," I whispered. "Pleasure and pain… You'd never been so deep. It just took me off guard."

He shook his head, letting me go then tracing a line between my breasts. "It was for the wrong reasons, Sarah. I wasn't trying to pleasure you."

"I don't think you were trying to hurt me either."

His lips trembled and he made a fist, pressing it against his forehead. "I couldn't tell you. I didn't want you to know. I didn't want you feeling bad."

"What are you talking about?" I held his shoulders, gently digging my fingers into his shirt.

"Blake," he croaked. "I should've been there for him that day. Instead of being the good brother, I left him because I wanted to be with you. While we were having sex, he was dying. Every time I touched you after that, I'd think of him." Justin's voice grew soft, like he was seeing it all again. His wide eyes stared straight through me. "You didn't see his eyes, the blood. He was supposed to be getting married that day."

"Justin." My voice was firm as I grabbed his face and forced his gaze to mine. "That was not your fault. Blake died because he was driving on the wrong side of the road without a helmet…and that other car was going too fast. That had nothing to do with you."

"I shouldn't have left him," he choked. His eyes were swamped with tears. "It was his wedding day, he was distracted. I could have saved his life."

Seeing Justin on the verge of tears set off my own. I sniffed and pressed my forehead against his. "Throwing away your life isn't going to bring him back. Don't destroy us because you feel guilty. Please, I need my husband back. You can't live the rest of your life like this."

"I know that in my head. That's why I'm here."

Smiling at his tear-soaked gaze, I whispered, "I'm going to make you believe it in your heart."

I planted my lips on his and kissed him with everything I had. Our lips shook against each other. Our salty tears mingled, but I wouldn't let him pull away.

With trembling fingers, I unbuttoned his shirt and tugged it off his body until there was nothing between us. Wrapping my arms around his neck, I crushed our naked torsos together and held on. It was like waiting for the jury to deliver their verdict. My heart thundered as I gave Justin the next move and prayed…prayed for his arms to glide around me, for him to take a risk.

I closed my eyes, letting the tears slip down my cheeks as I waited.

And then…

Very slowly…

My prayers were answered.

THIRTY-FOUR

JUSTIN

I ran the pads of my fingers over her skin, tracing the line of her ribs before traveling up her spine. She let out a shuddering sigh and squeezed tighter, spreading her hands over my back.

I released a ragged breath and met her strength, locking her against me. Burying my nose in her hair, I inhaled her scent. Memories fired through me—wistful, powerful, all-consuming. I let her coat my senses until my body was thrumming with one desire.

Lifting her up, I whipped us around so she was lying beneath me. Her eyes sparkled, matching the ring I'd slid onto her finger two years ago. We'd promised each other a life together then, having no idea a tornado was going to wipe us out. All we saw was a wedding in our future, a happy, perfect life together. We got the perfect wedding, and then…life happened.

I tugged her bathrobe and splayed it open so I could see her entire body.

"You are so beautiful," I whispered, running my hands across her smooth skin and marveling at each curve. She was soft, yet firm. Slender muscles beneath layers of silky white skin. I sucked her nipple into my mouth, enjoying the sound of her sweet whimper. A flash of Enrique touching her shot through my head. I bashed it away, my insides protesting with a feral growl. I squeezed her other breast, claiming her again, taking back what was rightfully mine.

Her mewls of pleasure kissed my brain, urging me to keep going. Sarah unbuttoned me, wrestling off my pants while I attended to her. Her breath hitched and caught as she moaned and tipped her head back. I rose to my knees, unwilling to release her as she finished undressing me.

The second I was naked, I lay on top of her. She spread her legs, forcing my throbbing cock against her thigh. Tipping her hips, she silently told me to get on with it. I ran my fingers down her body, squeezing her hip before weaving around between her legs.

My fingers slipped inside her—she was a hot, sweet mess. The second my mind registered her readiness, my hand got out of the way and I plunged into her.

She felt so damn good I nearly came on the spot. Clenching my jaw, I swallowed back my groan and pulled out, before thrusting into her again.

Sarah's sweet groans covered me. I looked down at her, smiling at the way her head tipped back, drinking in the shape her neck made as she buried her face in a pillow of blonde hair before craning back and biting her lower lip. She was the sexiest thing I'd ever seen.

I moved inside her again, finding our familiar rhythm. Grasping her firm butt, I coaxed her legs around my hips and drove into her, kissing the crook of her neck while she gripped my back and breathed into my ear.

"Justin," she whispered.

But I didn't hear her. I was back in England again, watching us do it on an old wooden desk. Then someone pressed fast-forward in my brain, and I was suddenly staring at my dead brother. His lifeless eyes and caved-in skull confronted me.

No. My mind protested, making my body buck and jerk. I thrust into my wife, hammering her body as I tried to escape my demons. They rose around me like tidal waves in a tossing ocean, smashing over me, taking me hostage while I tried to pleasure the one person who meant the most.

Like last time, I was transported to another place, my mind unable to control my body. All I could hear was distant grunting and a soft voice calling me.

"Justin."

I squeezed my eyes shut, willing myself back to that place.

"Justin, stop."

Sarah's voice hitched. A squealing of brakes crashed through my mind.

"Justin, stop!"

My eyes flashed open and I jerked away from her, rising up on my arms and trying to pull myself free. She locked me in place with her legs, crossing her ankles and digging her heels into my butt, keeping me inside.

I panted, my entire body trembling. "Let me go, Sarah. I'm not hurting you again."

"No, you're not." Her voice was calm, in contrast to mine. I wrestled against her, but she squeezed my arms so hard her nails dug into my flesh. Her thighs gripped my hips, holding them steady. "I'm yours, Justin. You can go as deep as you like…as long as you're not thinking about him. This moment right here belongs to us. I'm claiming it, and every moment after that." She grabbed my face, forcing me to look at her. "You are mine, Justin Doyle. You're *mine*. So, you just keep your eyes on me."

Her firm command sent a quiet ripple through me. My shoulder muscles slowly relaxed, then my back. Like knots unfurling, my taut body breathed a sigh of relief. Lowering myself to my elbows, I wound one of her blonde tendrils around my finger before pressing it against my lips. Sarah's erect nipples brushed across my chest, working like spark plugs to reignite me. I kept my eyes on hers, shifting slowly at first then increasing the tempo until I was gliding in and out of her. It was easy to keep the nightmares in check when I was looking into her eyes. They were like two guiding lights, steering me home.

I dove a little deeper, our breaths mingling together as the pressure built inside both of us. I could see her close to orgasm. Her hooded eyes glazed over, her fingers digging into my shoulders. Her whimpering breaths quickened while her hips tipped up, shifting the angle so I could plunge even deeper. Pushing up, I moved to my knees, holding her hips so she rose with me. Her arms slapped onto the mattress, clutching the covers as I buried myself inside her.

I could sense she wanted to close her eyes and drown in the sweet sensations riding through us, but she never did. She kept her gaze on me the whole time. A shock of pleasure so forceful it threatened to take me out coursed through me. Sarah's eyes flashed wide and she cried out, her muscles bunching as the orgasm rocked us both. I clutched her perfect ass and emptied myself into her until every ounce of energy was zapped from me.

And then everything went still, like the calm after a raging storm. A soft, gentle whisper of peace stirred inside me.

Sarah let out a deep, throaty giggle that told me she was satisfied. I flopped down beside her with a dopey grin, dragging her into my arms. She perched her head on her hand and gazed down at me, tracing the line of my lips.

"Welcome home," she whispered, her voice quivering over the words.

I tucked a lock of hair behind her ear. There were no words big enough for the emotion inside me, so I just stared at her, hoping she could read my mind.

Her gentle smile and the glistening in her eyes gave me hope that she could. With a little sniff, she pulled in a shaky breath and mouthed, "I love you."

"I love you too," I murmured then guided her head to my chest and nestled her against my body, right where she belonged.

THIRTY-FIVE

SARAH

A beam of light woke me.

It was shining directly across my face. I cracked one eye open and noticed I hadn't closed the curtains properly the night before. I rolled over with a soft groan and found myself face to face with the *right* man.

I smiled as a warm buzz radiated through my chest.

Justin was asleep. Soft breaths whistled between his lips as he lightly snored. I gently ran my finger over his dark eyebrow. His forehead was wrinkle free. I traced the smooth skin up to his hairline and threaded my fingers into his curls.

A grateful smile pushed my mouth even wider as that buzz shifted to a powerful force that swarmed my entire body. I loved him so much.

My wandering touch stirred him. He twitched and shifted, his strong hand landing on my hip and closing the gap between us.

I wriggled around and pressed my back against his naked torso. My butt couldn't help pressing against him, stirring his sleeping member. It hardened quickly, making me grin. Justin's hand tucked beneath my breast. He gave it a light squeeze while nuzzling my shoulders.

Closing my eyes with a blissful exhale, I relished the feel of his hard body behind me. Squeezing my nipple, he traced a line down to my waist, around my belly button then between my legs. My breath hitched as he found my sweet spot. I giggled then moaned as his strokes set my body alight. His hands knew me so well, and his deft touch had me quickly biting the pillow to muffle my lusty scream. I shuddered against him, my breathing punchy and erratic as the orgasm sizzled through me. Nudging my leg with his knee, he spread me open and slid straight home.

I lifted my arm over my head and clutched his curls as we rocked against each other. He took his time—a smooth, languid ride to ecstasy...and the perfect way to start a new day...a new dawn...a new era.

Wrapping his arms around me, he held me close and mumbled in my ear, "I want to wake up like that every day for the rest of my life."

I giggled and turned around so I could face him. Resting my hand on his cheek, I searched his eyes before finally whispering, "I'm so glad you said that. For a while there, I thought I'd lost you."

He swallowed. "I'm sorry."

"Not as sorry as I am." I bit my lips together, remorse washing my smile away.

"You weren't the only one to blame." He brushed his lips against mine. "And it's in the past now. That's where it needs to stay."

I nodded, my thick throat making it impossible to talk.

"Can I show you something?"

Curiosity widened my eyes, and I bobbed my head in answer.

He grinned and sat up, giving me a sweet shot of his ass. I smiled as he padded across the room naked and pulled the laptop out of his bag.

With a curious grin, I sat up, bunching the pillows behind me and covering myself with the sheet. He nestled down next to me and opened his computer. Resting my head on his shoulder, I watched him pull up a video clip.

"I made this on the plane," he murmured. "I just needed something to stop me from going crazy..." He glanced at me. "And I wanted to show you that I'm ready to move forward."

"Okay." I turned back to the screen, excited for a piece of Justin movie magic.

His finger quivered over the keypad then he clicked...and something beautiful happened.

"I Won't Give Up" by Jason Mraz kicked in. The guitar riff was the perfect backing track for the images popping up on the screen. Tears glassed over my eyes as I watched snippets from our wedding day—laughter, kisses, dreamy gazes as we danced in each other's arms. The shots then changed to pictures of us together in college. I recognized a couple of them from Justin's engagement video. We were so incredibly happy back then. We'd had something beautiful…and we were going to have it again.

The images shifted to pictures I didn't recognize. There was one of a small apartment then images of wedding dresses, flowers, shoes, cakes, photos, venues. My forehead crinkled until the screen went black and the words popped up: I … want … to … make … your … dreams … come … true.

I covered my mouth and sucked in a gasp. My wedding business, the one I'd given up on without even realizing it.

The song finished, and I turned to him with wide eyes.

"What are you saying right now?"

He closed his laptop and placed it aside before turning to me. Taking both my hands, he rubbed his thumbs over my knuckles and started talking.

"When I first asked you to marry me, I thought our life was going to be perfect. Everything fell into place so easily—the wedding, the house, the jobs. But then we got hit by this massive tsunami that neither of us saw coming. We were so unprepared. All the dreams we'd had, everything we thought we'd become got pushed aside as we tried to survive." His face bunched with regret. "I didn't let you in. I drove you away from me." He raised my hand to his lips and brushed my knuckles. "But as much as I've hated it, I wouldn't take any of it back. We've still got a long way to go, Sparks, but if this has taught me anything, it's that life isn't perfect. We're still going to have some rough times, but in the midst of all that, I know for certain that I want you by my side. No matter what happens, I want to help you make your dreams come true."

His eyes warmed with a smile.

"We've been doing this all wrong. I should never have taken that job with your dad. I should have told you I didn't want it. And even though this job for Echelon has taught you so much, you don't need it. You are talented enough to stand on your own two feet. You don't need Enrique DeMarco's name behind you. We can do this. We can have the wedding business you've always dreamed of. Why wait? Let's take a risk and do it now, together."

I squeezed his hands. "Together?"

"Yeah. I had eleven hours to think about it on the plane. We don't have to be big and famous. We can start out small, offer couples affordable wedding packages. You design the dresses and the theme. We find venues, hire caterers for them, work with freelance photographers. I can put together wedding albums, videos, design invitations. We can take care of the business together. We've always been the perfect pair. Let's prove it to the world. Let's prove it to ourselves."

My mouth wouldn't close. I was too in awe of my husband to do anything more than give him a breathy giggle. Justin was back, but better. There was a determination and confidence coursing out of him that I'd never seen before.

"I…"

He grinned. "You love it."

"I do!" I threw my arms around him and jumped into his lap with a squeal.

His chest vibrated with a chuckle as I kissed his neck and face.

Out of breath, I pulled back and looked him in the eye. "I want to move out of that house in Pacific Palisades."

"Me too." He tipped his head back. "I've never liked it."

"Me neither!" I let out a delighted laugh. "I just want to find *our* place. I want to find us. We've always been surrounded with other people. We've never had to make it on our own. You followed Blake, and when he was gone, you were lost. I tried to become the perfect designer and ended up failing in the one thing most important to me." I caught my breath then blew out a thoughtful sigh. "I just want to love you, and be with you… Build a life with you."

Justin ran his fingers up my back and over my shoulder to cup the side of my face. His fingers pressed into my neck, and he pulled me toward him.

And then, after a slow, languid kiss, Justin *did*

make all my dreams come true when he said, "Always. I promise you, no matter what, I won't give up on us."

I smiled and sang the first line of "Rough Water." He didn't smile like I expected him to. Instead, he brushed his fingers down my face and whispered, "Never again. I'll never let you go again."

THIRTY-SIX

JUSTIN

I held Sarah's hand as we gazed up at the Eiffel Tower. The sun, having shone so brightly all morning, decided to take the afternoon off. Puffy clouds, tinted gray, were hovering above us, threatening rain. We had no umbrella, but neither of us seemed in a rush to head back to the hotel.

Sarah was supposed to be fussing around backstage at a fashion show, but having quit, she decided to bail. She checked in with Julian, and he said he'd cover it. He was too busy and flustered to ask too many questions.

Once the call had been made, Sarah flopped

onto the bed and cried. I had to prepare myself for that. Just because we'd decided not to quit on our marriage didn't mean we'd be free of working through the aftermath of Blake's death and Sarah's one-night stand.

But I'd let her in on my dark secret and already I felt the shift inside me. She was right—I just had to keep my eyes on her. I glanced down as she lifted her phone and took another shot of the tower. She was wearing her white denim skirt with the tattered edging and a powder blue tank. She'd matched it with her favorite pair of blue and white Skechers. Her long hair hung loose around her shoulders, and her only jewelry was the two rings that told the world she was mine.

Sarah studied the picture on her phone screen. "Even in gray skies, it's pretty."

"Some things are beautiful no matter what the conditions." I stared at her the whole time I said it.

Her cheeks rose with a smile and she wrinkled her nose.

I squeezed her hand then turned back to the tower. I'd always wanted to visit Paris. Under different circumstances would have been nice, but winning your wife back fell into the epic category, so I'd take it.

We were still worried about our future. So many unknowns and changes ahead—moving house, setting up a business. I had some savings set aside, but we'd still need to borrow some money to really kick things off. It was all so huge and overwhelming, but we had to try. We had to break free of where we'd been. We had to start afresh.

"I've got an idea," I murmured.

Her eyes were large and bright when she looked up at me. "What's that?"

A light rain started falling. It was more mist than raindrops, the kind of sprinkling that tickled the skin and kissed your clothing.

I grinned, tugging her along the large concrete area in front of the tower. Thanks to the weather, it was sparsely populated.

"We're in Paris."

"We are." Sarah slipped her phone back into her handbag.

I stopped a few steps later and turned, drawing her against me and threading my fingers behind her lower back. "It's beautiful."

She rested her hands on my arms and smiled. "It is."

"We're in love."

"Forever," she promised.

I pursed my lips and looked up at the tower then back down at her. "So, let's make this our new wedding anniversary. Let's pretend that today is the first day of our lives together."

Her mouth broke into the kind of smile that could knock a guy on his ass. I held on to her, relishing its light as she nodded. "I like that."

Clearing my throat with just a touch of pride, I pulled my phone free. The lyrics from our engagement video whistled through my brain, and I decided that since this was our new wedding anniversary, I needed to do something pretty damn romantic.

"Are we taking our new wedding photos?" Sarah leaned against my chest, already posing for a selfie.

"In a minute." I grinned. "First, I want to dance with you in the rain."

Finding the perfect song, I pressed Play and turned up the volume before slipping it back in my pocket.

Sarah's eyes sparkled as soon as she heard "All About Us" start to play. I stepped back and reached out my hand. With a twinkling smile, she placed hers in mine. I gently squeezed her fingers then raised her hand over her head so she could spin beneath my arm. With a little giggle, she turned back to face me, and we assumed the waltzing position. It was our first dance in the rain...right in front of the Eiffel Tower.

People stopped to watch us. A group of Chinese tourists started to laugh and snapped a few photos. We didn't even care. All we saw was each other. It was the beginning of something new. It wouldn't be perfect, and we'd have our ups and our downs...but we'd be in it together. And that's all that mattered.

EPILOGUE

SARAH

"Okay, so you like it?" I asked, my nose wrinkling without my say-so.

"Uh, yeah!" Kelly couldn't take her eyes off my drawing. Having met with her the week before, I had a pretty good idea what she was hoping for in a wedding dress, but it was nice to see I'd surpassed her expectations. "It's so beautiful." She touched the pencil sketch, tracing the line of the bodice. "I'm going to look amazing."

"You could walk down the aisle in a paper sack and you'd look amazing," Marcus piped up from the other side of the room. He was hovering over

Justin's computer, talking business...while eavesdropping on our conversation.

Kelly's cheeks flared with color and she winked at me then bit her lip before gazing back at the design with a dreamy smile. I'd spent hours lovingly putting the sketches together, dreaming up different fabrics and cuts to accentuate Kelly's figure. It would be nothing but a pleasure to arrange Kelly and Marcus's wedding for them. They were the first clients of *All About The Bride and Groom*, but Kelly had already promised more business. Two of her bridesmaids were both getting married, and they all had friends who were in the wedding stage of their lives. If we pulled this off and made Marcus and Kelly's the wedding of the year, we'd be sure to pick up more clientele.

The last few weeks had been insane. We'd touched down in LA and hit the ground running. Within three days, we'd found a tiny apartment and boxed up all our stuff. We'd then flown to New Mexico to tell Justin's parents about our plans. He had expected them to be disappointed in his decision, but when we talked it through, they eventually came around to wishing us luck and offering to help us get started.

We decided not to take their financial offer. We'd made a commitment to do this thing on our own, and although family support was helpful, we didn't want to be tied to anyone but each other.

Dealing with my parents was a much harder task, but we stuck to our guns and moved out of their place the day after we returned from

Albuquerque. Our new apartment was seriously tiny, but we turned the upstairs loft area into our bedroom, hid the pokey kitchen behind a screen, and set up our living and dining area as *All About The Bride and Groom* central.

With Marcus and Kelly's deposit, we were able to get the ball rolling on their wedding plans. So far, we'd found them the perfect venue, conceptualized the right theme, and were well on our way to creating *their* dream wedding. It was great to be able to test the waters on such awesome people. We'd met three times already to go over their ideas, making sure what they wanted was central to everything. The conversations had helped Justin and me put together questionnaires that would cover all the needs and wants of a couple preparing for their big day. Thanks to Justin's training, he was able to draw up contracts that would protect both us and the couples we were working with. Clay had been nice enough to give them the once-over.

Justin and I were committed to listening to the couple above all. If they wanted something crazy, then we'd make it happen for them. We knew all too well the pressure of pleasing everyone around them. Weddings were supposed to be about the bride and groom, not everybody else.

Pulling a shoebox out from under the table, I glanced over my shoulder to make sure the guys weren't watching before placing it in front of Kelly. I lifted out the first swatch of fabric and set it next to the picture. It was a square of Prussian blue silk.

Over it, I placed a swatch of white lace, intricately woven with twisting stems and closed rosebuds.

"I was thinking of this for you. I know it breaks the norm, but this blue would look so amazing with your skin tone, and it'll bring out the color of your eyes. The white overlay softens the darkness, but it will look so stunning if you pair it with a bunch of white and blue roses. Simple round bouquet, nothing fancy. And then I was thinking makeup-wise, we could go for the smoky eyes and then a sparkling, glitter lipstick." I pointed to my sketch of the dress with my pinky finger. "With this neckline, you don't need too much jewelry. I was thinking a simple diamond bracelet and earrings, nothing more. Hair up, something classy like a French roll…and no veil. We'll put some sparkles in your hair…or maybe a few baby rosebuds to match the bouquet." I was talking quietly so the boys wouldn't hear me. I probably shouldn't have been discussing the dress with Marcus in the room, but I was too excited not to show Kelly what I'd dreamed up.

She blinked a couple of times then looked at me with her wide eyes and started nodding. "I love it."

"Really?"

"Yes." She wrapped her arms around me, pulling me into a choking hug. I giggled and patted her back as she squealed in my ear. So very un-Kelly DeMarco.

I pulled away from her and laughed some more. Her cheeks were flushed, her eyes dancing. "I love how different and untraditional it is."

"How different what is?" Marcus stood straight and spun to face us.

"Nothing!" we said in unison, diving in front of the fabric so he couldn't see.

He rolled his eyes and turned back to Justin. "It's not bad luck to see you in your dress before the wedding. I don't believe in that crap."

"Maybe so, but don't go stealing my surprise," Kelly quipped. "I want you to be so blown away by my beauty that you'll lose the ability to think straight."

He looked over his shoulder and grinned. "Happens every time I open my eyes in the morning, baby."

"Yeah, right." Kelly rolled her eyes and spun back to pick up the fabric. Her lips rose into a dreamy smile, and I couldn't work out if she was picturing herself in the dress or still a little giddy over Marcus's sweet sentiments. Maybe it was a little of both.

I rested my elbows on my workbench and clasped my fingers together.

This was going to be the best job ever— surrounded by couples in love while working with the man I loved. Yeah, we'd probably encounter a few bridezillas along the way, but we could work through that. I was pretty sure we could work through anything.

I turned to find Justin's eyes on me. His affectionate gaze warmed me from my ponytail to the tips of my toes. I bit my lip and winked at him. He winked back then returned to his computer screen, showing Marcus the idea he'd had for the invitations.

An hour later, I'd taken all of Kelly's measurements and we'd gotten their approval on the wedding invites. I flopped into the chair next to Justin and pointed at our "To Do" list on his screen.

"You can tick that off as well." I pointed at *Approve bridesmaids' designs.* I'd shown those to Kelly after she'd stopped swooning over her dress. She loved my ideas for that too, only wanting to tweak a few suggestions I'd put forward. If things kept going at the rate they were, our first wedding job would be a breeze.

"I'm loving this." Justin let out a contended sigh.

"Me too." I grinned. "I know it's not always going to be this easy, but oh man, it's such a good start!"

Justin chuckled and pulled me into his lap. "It's good because it's ours. This is going to be great, Sparks. I've already gotten a call from Kelly's friend, Isla. She'll be bringing her soon-to-be husband over tomorrow."

"No way!" I gripped his shoulders. "This is really happening."

"It really is."

Our smiles pressed together as we took a short "kiss me" break. We'd been enjoying quite a few of those throughout the process, and it was only helping our business. Well, it was in my opinion anyway.

The alarm on my phone started buzzing. I let it ring a few times before reluctantly leaving Justin's lap to turn it off.

"I better go get Jane." I sighed, still worried about what I might find. She'd left for England to go and discover herself. I only hoped she'd found what she was looking for. I was anxious to see her, yet hesitant as well. She'd dropped offline while she was away, merely updating me with brief texts and the odd email. I'd been so focused on reorganizing my life, I'd let her aloofness slip by and felt like a bad friend because of it.

Justin and I were finally back on track again, and I wondered how that might affect my relationship with Jane. She said she'd never be able to fall in love again, but would she be jealous or hesitant to hang around now that Justin and I were loved-up once more?

I couldn't imagine looking at a future with no one by my side. It'd be such a lonely road for her. I was determined to be the friend she needed, but I wasn't above pushing her in the right direction if I found a guy worthy of her.

My eyes skirted over Justin as I collected my things. How would he feel about Blake's one true love meeting someone else? It could potentially be really awkward, but I had to keep the bigger picture in mind. Jane was my best friend. If she returned from her self-discovery trip with some big, life-changing revelation, then so be it. But if she walked off that plane as the lonely girl I expected, then I was going to work.

The beauty of being in love far outweighed a life of solitude. Jane needed a man, and I was going to find her one.

Clearing my throat, I decided not to say anything to Justin until I'd assessed Jane's emotional state. I had the entire drive home from the airport to analyze her.

Swinging my bag onto my shoulder, I swayed over to my husband and straddled him. My skirt rode up past my butt with the help of his deft fingers. Squeezing my cheeks, he rubbed me over his crotch with a playful smile. "We should do this when you get back."

"Minus the clothes," I murmured against his lips.

He chuckled and held the back of my head, deepening the kiss and giving my senses a small preview of things to come.

I gripped his curls and rocked against him, enjoying the sheer pleasure of making out in the middle of the day. I had to go get my friend, but five minutes playing "tongue twister" with my man was exactly what newlyweds were supposed to do.

And that's what Justin and I were.

Newlyweds.

We'd had a two-night honeymoon in Paris then flew home to LA to start afresh in a marriage that neither of us was willing to give up on.

THE END

Thank you so much for reading *Rough Water*. If you've enjoyed it and would like to show me some support, please consider leaving a review on the site you purchased this book from.

KEEP READING TO FIND OUT ABOUT THE NEXT SONGBIRD NOVEL…

The next Songbird Novel belongs to:

Jane & Harry

GERONIMO

Due for release in summer 2016

Jane is on a mission of self-discovery. Having lost the love of her life in a horrific motorcycle accident on their wedding day, she's been a shell of the woman she once was. Learning to live without Blake is going to take more than just waking up each morning. So, she leaves for England to return to the place it all ended, in the hopes of figuring out how to negotiate life on her own. What she doesn't expect is to meet Harry Tindal, and for the hunky Brit to present her with a surprising proposition.

Harry never intended to approach the red-haired beauty when she stepped into the pub, but the music drew his feet her way. Before he knew it, he'd struck up a conversation with the fascinating woman, only to discover they were on similar missions. Trying to escape his painful past, Harry decides to step out of his comfort zone and invite Jane to join him for a fortnight of no regrets.

"No sex. No histories. No awkward conversations. Just two people living life to the max for two weeks. Then we say adios, thanks for a good time, and go our

separate ways."

Jane can't resist, and the couple embarks on a journey of faith that soon turns into something neither of them expected. As hearts unfurl, truths rise to the surface and the couple must decide if they're able to risk love once more and hand their hearts to someone new.

You can find the other Songbird Novels on Amazon.

FEVER
Ella & Cole's story

BULLETPROOF
Morgan & Sean's story

EVERYTHING
Jody & Leo's story

HOME
Rachel & Josh's story

TRUE LOVE
Nessa & Jimmy's story

TROUBLEMAKER
Marcus & Kelly's story

.

NOTE FROM THE AUTHOR

This has been a tough story to write. Heartache hurts, and broken love can be one of the hardest things to overcome. Sarah and Justin's story is soaked in sadness. I cried many tears while writing it.

So, why did I want to write such a book? Why explore such a sensitive topic?

I guess I wanted to unpack the idea that love doesn't need to be perfect to work…and that good things can come out of bad situations.

Sorrow can teach us so much. It's certainly taught me a thing or two. And I always find it so amazing how bright the light can be after you've waded through the darkness. Suffering makes us appreciate the good times that much more.

Thank you for sticking with Justin and Sarah, for not giving up when things looked so hopeless for them. Thank you for giving them time to work through their pain, for walking with them as they forgave each other…and themselves. I wanted this story to be about overcoming our deepest fears and choosing to become the kind of person we want to be.

Sometimes love does need to be a choice.

I hope this book has touched you in some way…tugged on your heartstrings just a little. It's such a privilege to write these Songbird novels. Thank you for letting me explore the complexities of love…and allowing me to accompany these journeys with songs that have touched my heart.

xx
Melissa

Keep reading for the playlist and the link to find it on Spotify.

ROUGH WATER SOUNDTRACK

(Please note: The songs listed below are not always the original versions, but the ones I chose to listen to while constructing this book. The songs are listed in the order they appear.)

ANGEL
Performed by Casting Crowns

SHE'S GOT A WAY
Performed by Billy Joel

YOUR BODY IS A WONDERLAND
Performed by John Mayer

ROUGH WATER
Performed by Travie McCoy and Jazon Mraz

I SEE YOU
Performed by Mika

GOOD GUYS
Performed by Mika

EMILY
Performed by Mika

GIRL PUT YOUR RECORDS ON
Performed by The Alley Cats

MELISSA PEARL

DON'T KNOW WHY
Performed by Norah Jones

WHERE I BELONG
Performed by Lindsey Ray

BULLETPROOF WEEKS
Performed by Matt Nathanson

HELLO
Performed by Adele

AIN'T NO SUNSHINE
Performed by Joan Osborne

I LOVE YOU ALWAYS FOREVER
Performed by Donna Lewis

THE BOOK OF LOVE
Performed by Gavin James

QUIET
Performed by Jason Mraz

I LOVE THE WAY YOU LOVE ME
Performed by Boyzone

WITHOUT YOU
Performed by Boyce Avenue

SAY SOMETHING
Performed by Pentatonix

NOT JUST YOU
Performed by Ebony Day

ONE CALL AWAY
Performed by Charlie Puth

DISTANCE
Performed by Christina Perri and Jason Mraz

CONFESSION
Performed by Florida Georgia Line

HAPPY ENDING
Performed by Mika

I WON'T GIVE UP
Performed by Jason Mraz

ALL ABOUT US
Performed by He Is We and Owl City

To enhance your reading experience, you can listen along to the playlist for ROUGH WATER on Spotify.
https://open.spotify.com/user/12146962946/playlist/2LsYyXUeovQwWfLPoKofT5

ACKNOWLEDGEMENTS

Creating a book is most definitely a group effort. I'd like to especially thank:

My critique readers: Cassie and Rae. This book was really hard to construct. Thank you so much for helping me get the story right.

My editor: Laurie. Once again, your edits and advice have been invaluable.

My proofreaders: I so appreciate your time and attention.

My advanced reading team: Thanks for the love. It means the world to me how much you enjoy the Songbird Novels.

My cover designer and photographer: Regina. This image is perfect...like you shot it just for this book. Thank you for once again creating magic.

My fellow writers: Inklings and Indie Inked. Thanks for your constant support and encouragement.

My fan club and readers: THANK YOU! I love and appreciate you guys so much.

My Mika buddy: Nadine - thank you for

introducing me to this amazing artist…and thank you for being my singing buddy and kindred spirit. I love you.

My family: You are my constant source of love and encouragement. Thank you.

My savior: Thank you for choosing us. For sacrificing everything so we could glimpse how real and perfect your love is.

OTHER BOOKS BY MELISSA PEARL

The Songbird Novels
Fever—Bulletproof—Everything—Home—True
Love—Troublemaker—Rough Water
Coming in summer 2016: Geronimo

The Space Between Heartbeats
Plus two novellas: The Space Before & The Space
Beyond

The Fugitive Series
I Know Lucy — Set Me Free

The Masks Series
True Colors — Two-Faced— Snake Eyes — Poker
Face

The Time Spirit Trilogy
Golden Blood — Black Blood — Pure Blood

The Elements Trilogy
Unknown — Unseen — Unleashed

The Mica & Lexy Series
Forbidden Territory—Forbidden Waters

Find out more on Melissa Pearl's website:
www.melissapearlauthor.com

ABOUT MELISSA PEARL

Melissa Pearl is a kiwi at heart but currently lives in Suzhou, China with her husband and two sons. She trained as an elementary school teacher but has always had a passion for writing and finally completed her first manuscript in 2003. She has been writing ever since, and the more she learns, the more she loves it.

She writes young adult and new adult fiction in a variety of romance genres—paranormal, fantasy, suspense, and contemporary. Her goal as a writer is to give readers the pleasure of escaping their everyday lives for a while and losing themselves in a journey…one that will make them laugh, cry, and swoon.

MELISSA PEARL ONLINE

Website:
www.melissapearlauthor.com

YouTube Channel:
www.youtube.com / user / melissapearlauthor

Facebook:
www.facebook.com / melissapearlauthor

Instagram:
instagram.com / melissapearlauthor

Twitter:
twitter.com / MelissaPearlG

Pinterest:
www.pinterest.com / melissapearlg

CPSIA information can be obtained
at www.ICGtesting.com
Printed in the USA
LVOW10s0230041116
511637LV00001B/35/P